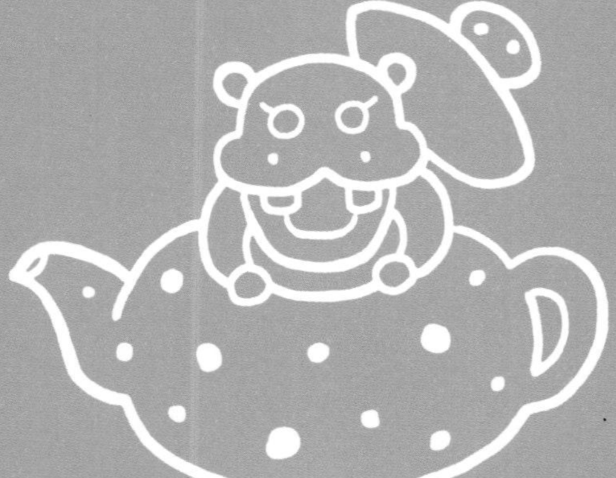

Aggretsuko™

Down the Rabbit Hole

ONI PRESS
AN ONI PRESS PUBLICATION

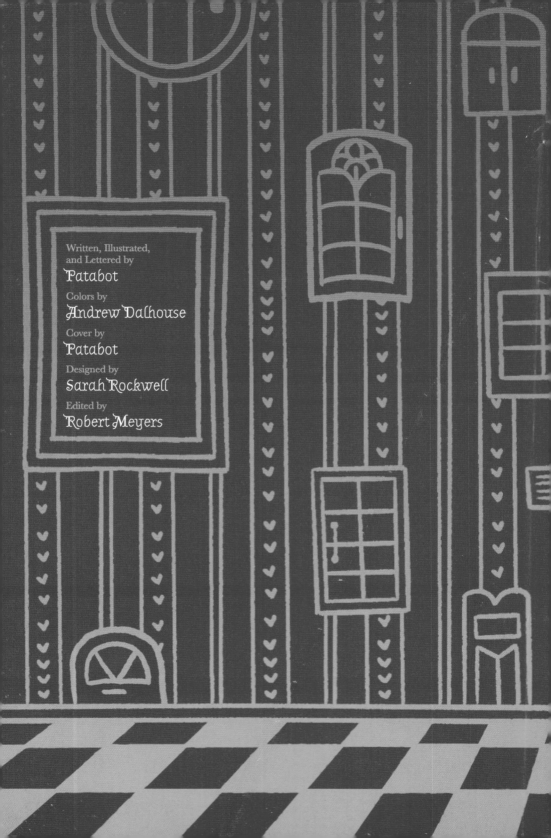

Written, Illustrated,
and Lettered by
Patabot

Colors by
Andrew Dalhouse

Cover by
Patabot

Designed by
Sarah Rockwell

Edited by
Robert Meyers

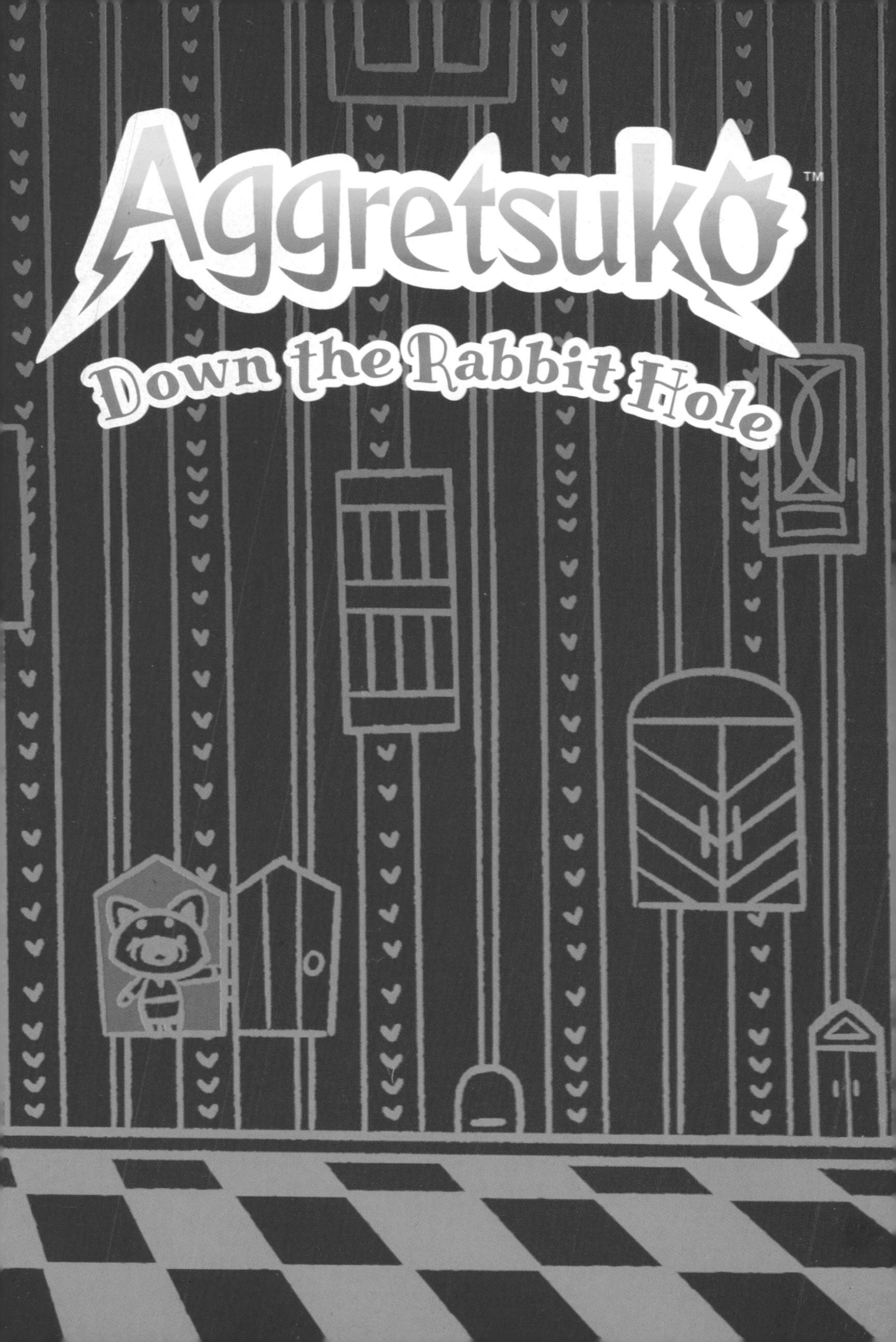
Aggretsuko™
Down the Rabbit Hole

published by oni-lion forge publishing group, llc
James Lucas Jones, *president & publisher* Sarah Gaydos, *editor in chief* Charlie Chu, *e.v.p. of creative & business development* Brad Rooks, *director of operations* Amber O'Neill, *special projects manager* Margot Wood, *director of marketing & sales* Katie Sainz, *marketing manager* Tara Lehmann, *publicist* Holly Aitchison, *consumer marketing manager* Troy Look, *director of design & production* Kate Z. Stone, *senior graphic designer* Hilary Thompson, *graphic designer* Sarah Rockwell, *graphic designer* Angie Knowles, *digital prepress lead* Vincent Kukua, *digital prepress technician* Jasmine Amiri, *senior editor* Shawna Gore, *senior editor* Amanda Meadows, *senior editor* Robert Meyers, *senior editor, licensing* Desiree Rodriguez, *editor* Grace Bornhoft, *editor* Zack Soto, *editor* Chris Cerasi, *editorial coordinator* Steve Ellis, *vice president of games* Ben Eisner, *game developer* Michelle Nguyen, *executive assistant* Jung Lee, *logistics coordinator* Joe Nozemack, *publisher emeritus*

Special thanks to:
Cindy Suzuki, Jeff Parker, Marjorie Santos, Susan Zhang, Susan Tran, and Linh Forse for their invaluable assistance.

ONI PRESS

onipress.com
@onipress

lionforge.com
@lionforge

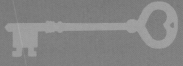

sanrio.com
@sanrio
@aggretsuko
aggretsuko
@aggretsuko
aggretsuko

Aggretsuko™ by Sanrio®

First Edition: October 2021
ISBN 978-1-62010-977-9
eISBN 978-1-63715-010-8

Printing numbers:
1 3 5 7 9 10 8 6 4 2

Library of Congress Control Number 2021934312

Printed in China.

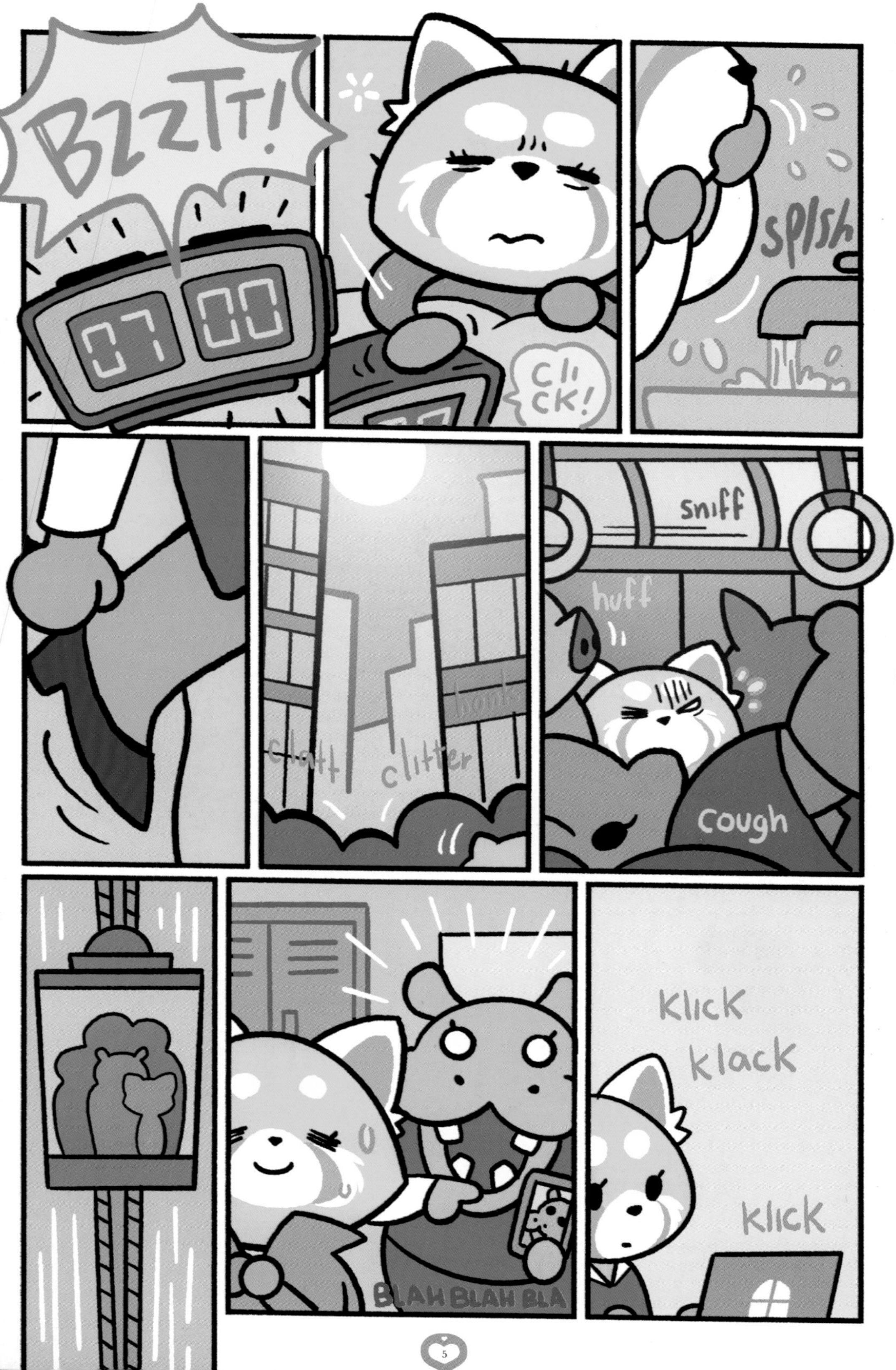
BZZTT!
CLICK!
splsh
sniff
huff
cough
honk
clatt
clitter
BLAH BLAH BLA
klick
klack
klick

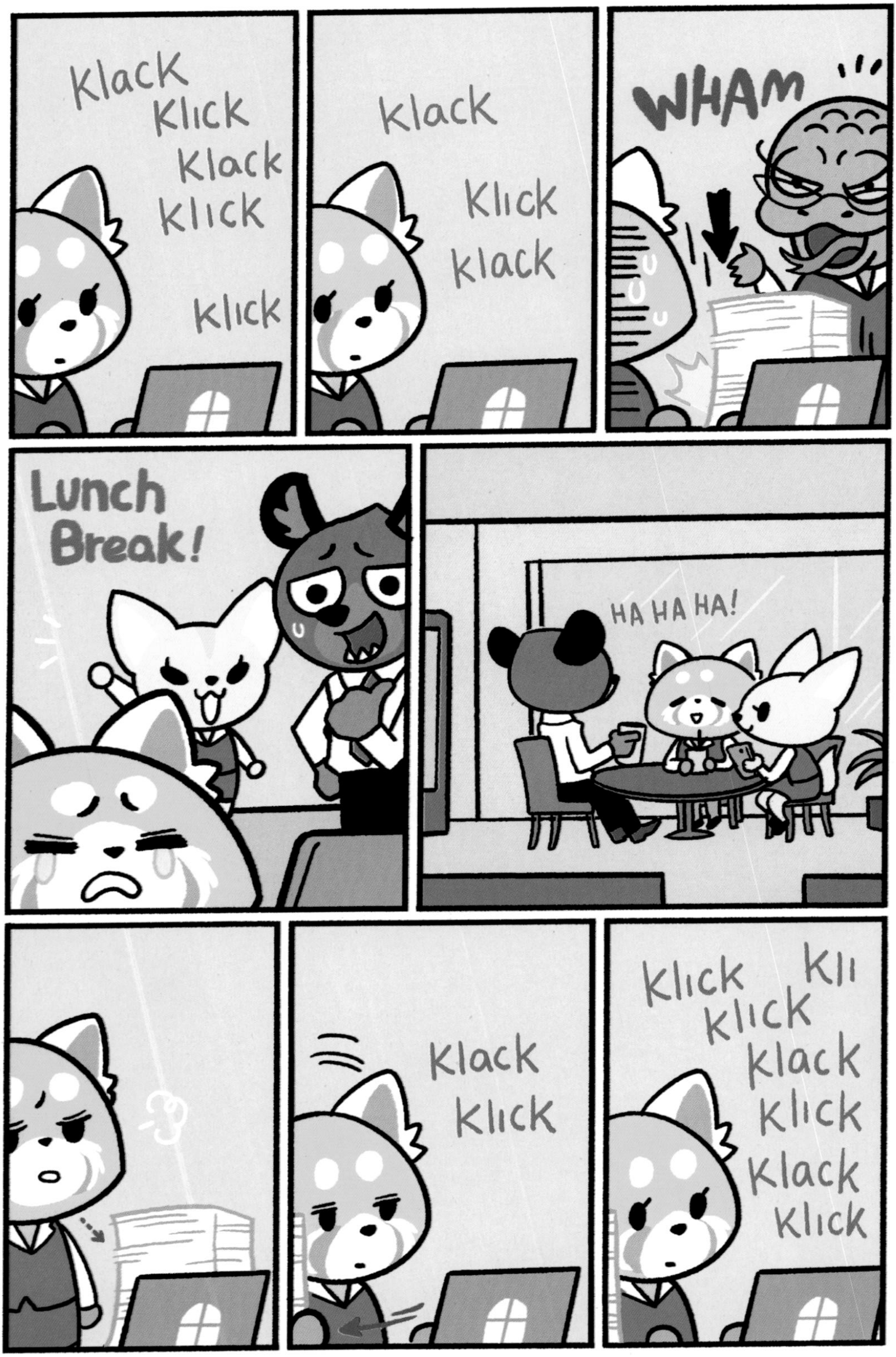
Klack
Klick
Klack
Klick
Klick
Klack
Klick
Klack
WHAM
Lunch Break!
HA HA HA!
Klack
Klick
Klick
Klick
Klack
Klick
Klack
Klick

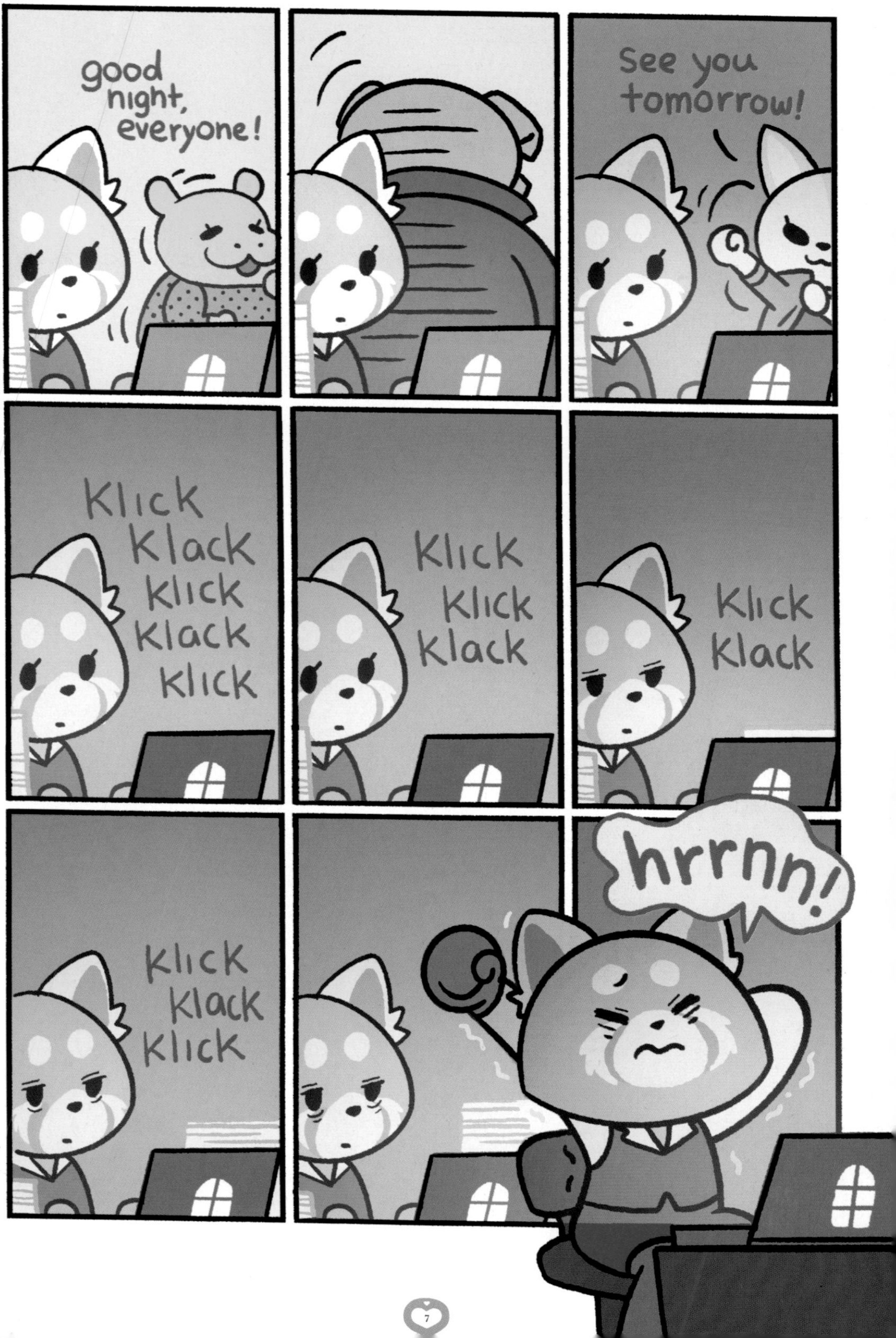
good night, everyone!
See you tomorrow!
Klick Klack klick Klack klick
Klick Klick Klack
Klick Klack
Klick Klack Klick
hrrnn!

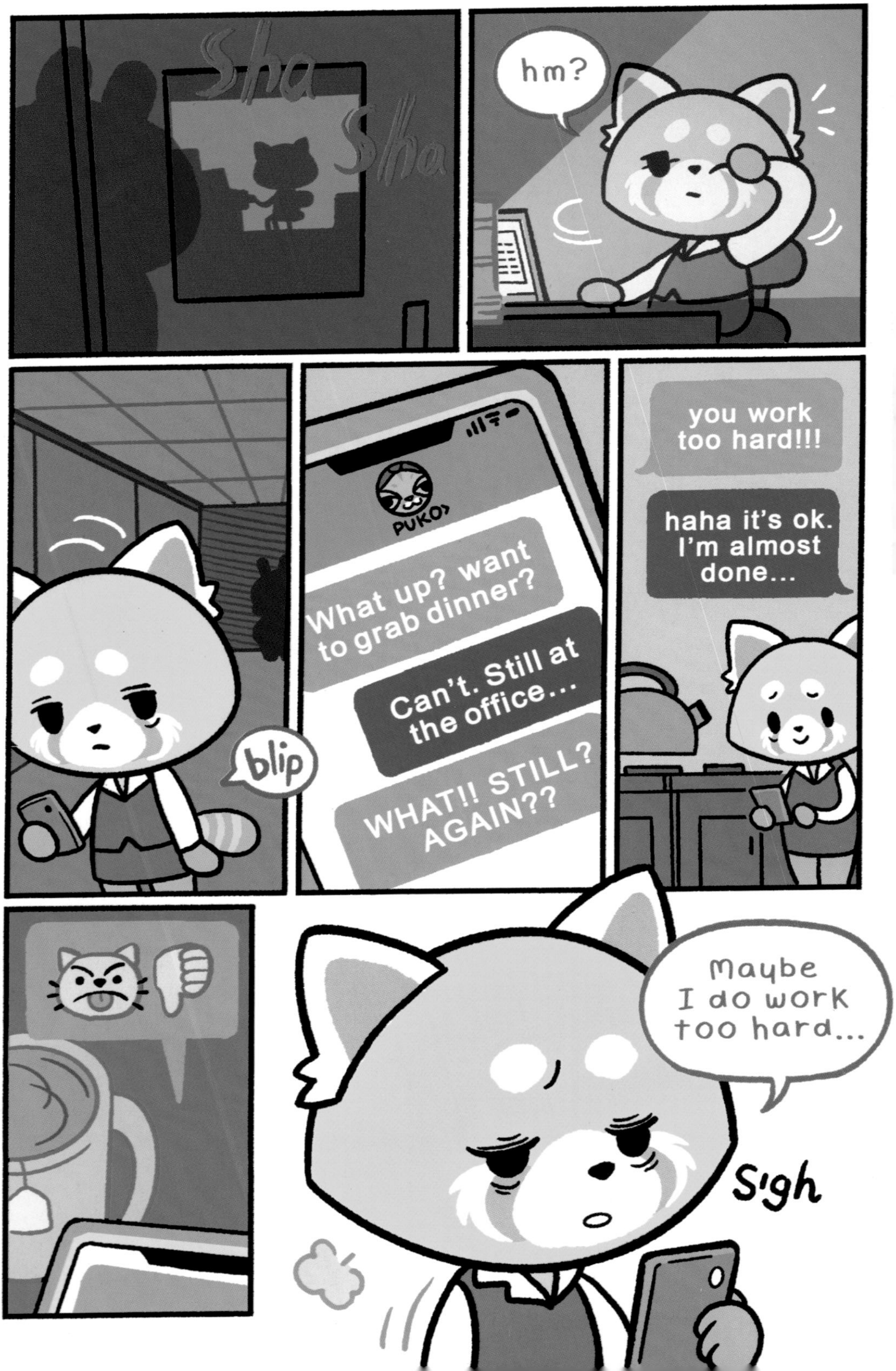
Sha
Sha
hm?
blip
PUKO
What up? want to grab dinner?
Can't. Still at the office...
WHAT!! STILL? AGAIN??
you work too hard!!!
haha it's ok. I'm almost done...
Maybe I do work too hard...
Sigh

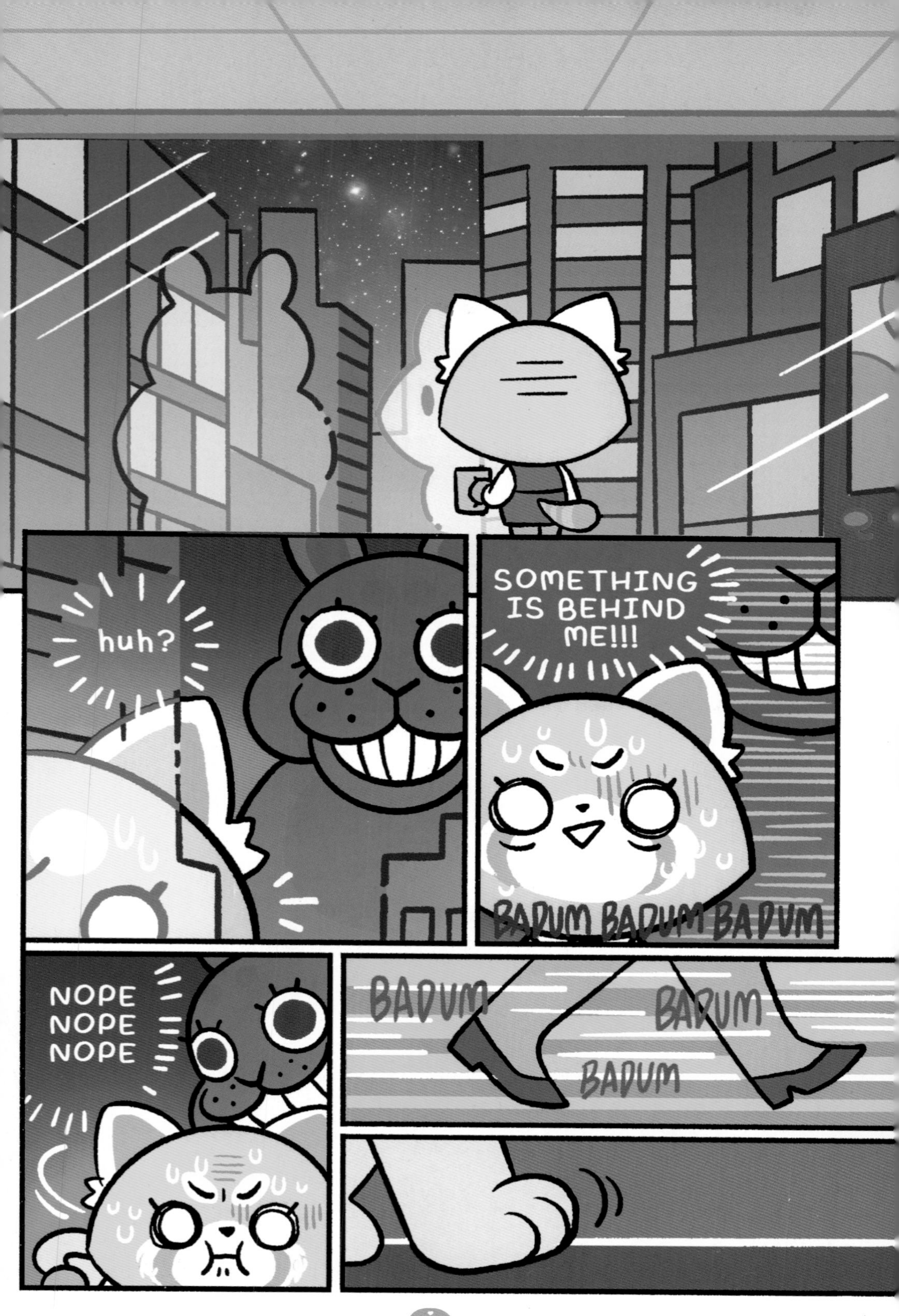
huh?
SOMETHING IS BEHIND ME!!!
BADUM BADUM BADUM
NOPE NOPE NOPE
BADUM
BADUM
BADUM

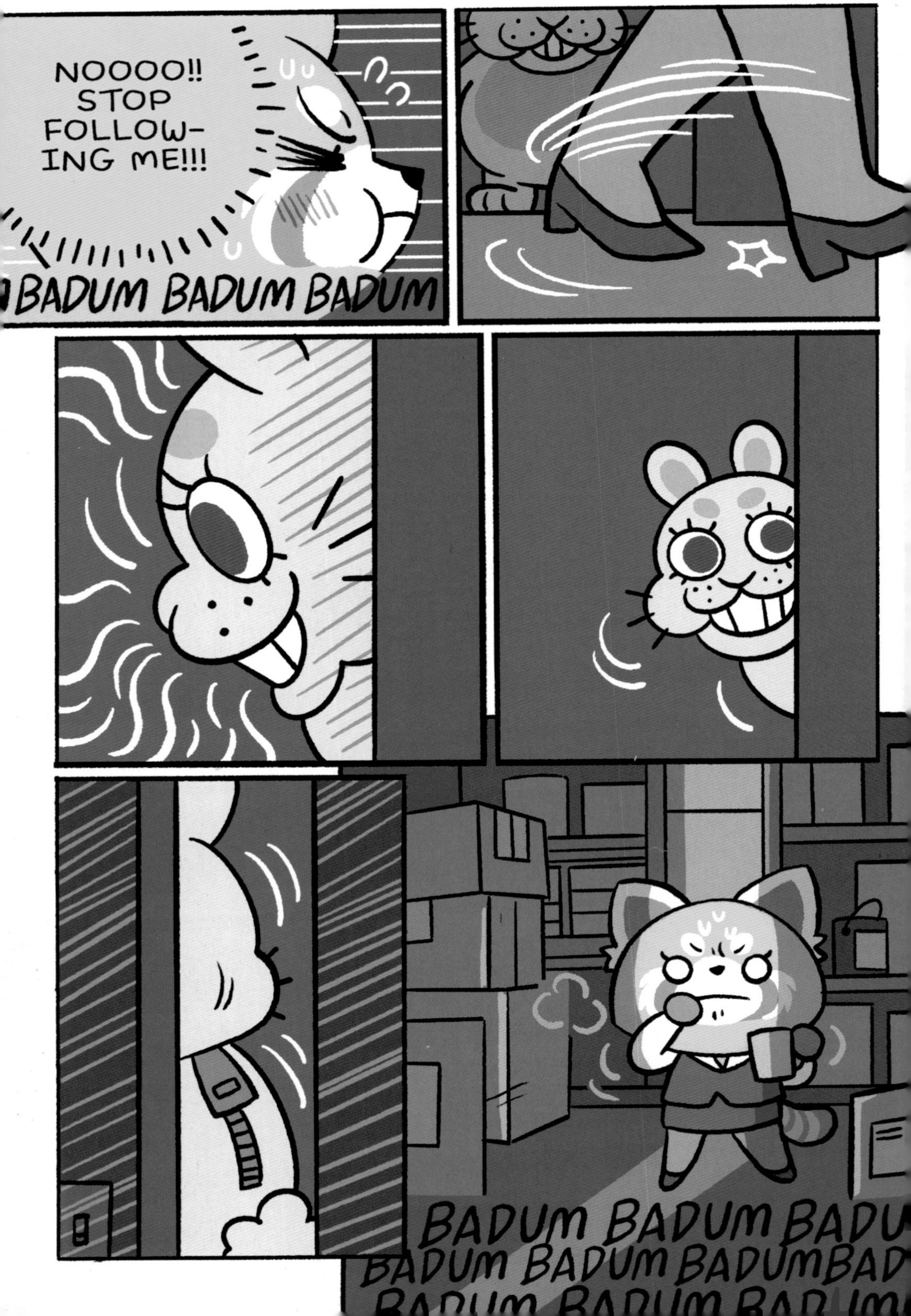
NOOOO!! STOP FOLLOW-ING ME!!!
BADUM BADUM BADUM
BADUM BADUM
BADUM BADUM BADUM

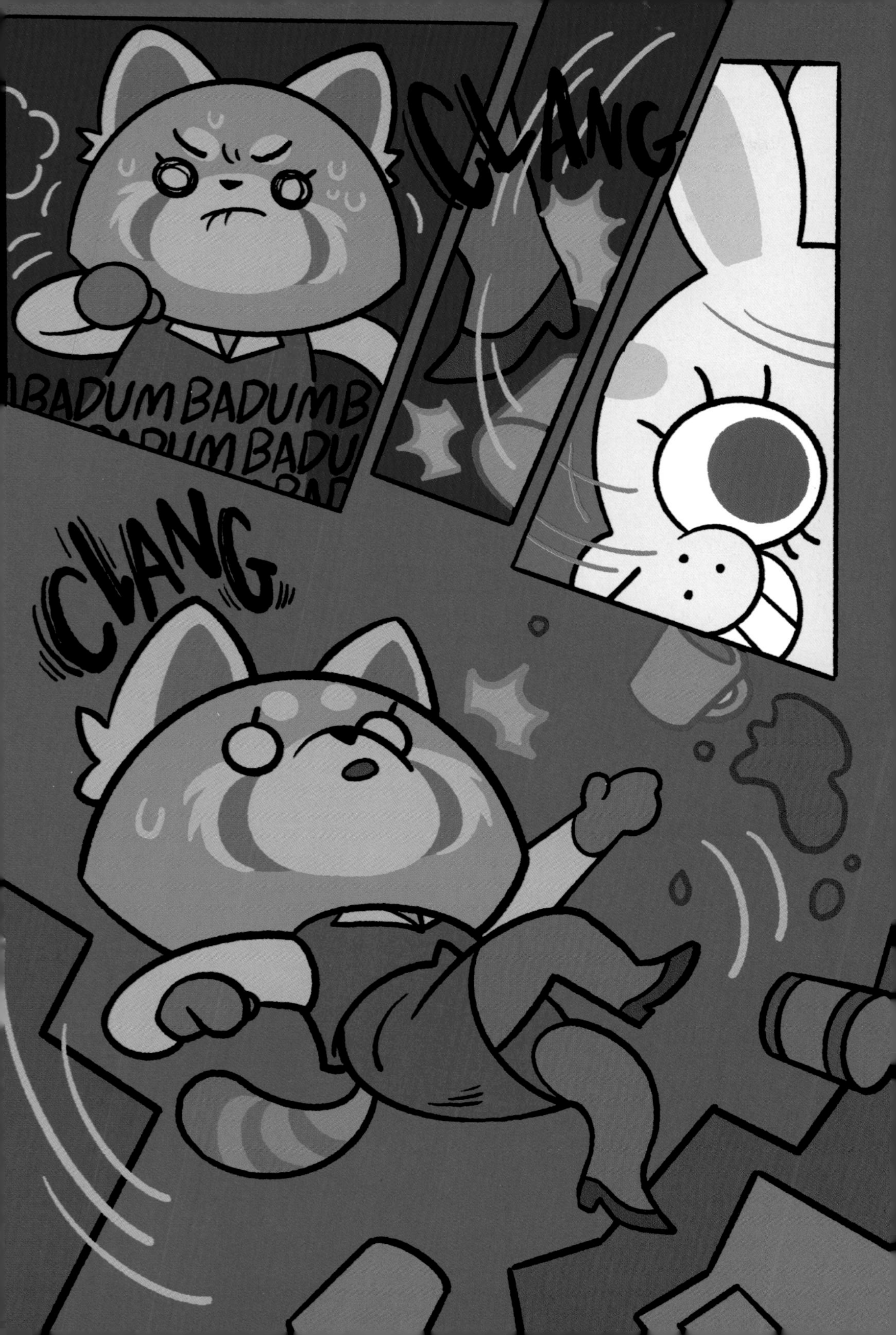
BADUM BADUM BADUM BADUM
CLANG
CLANG

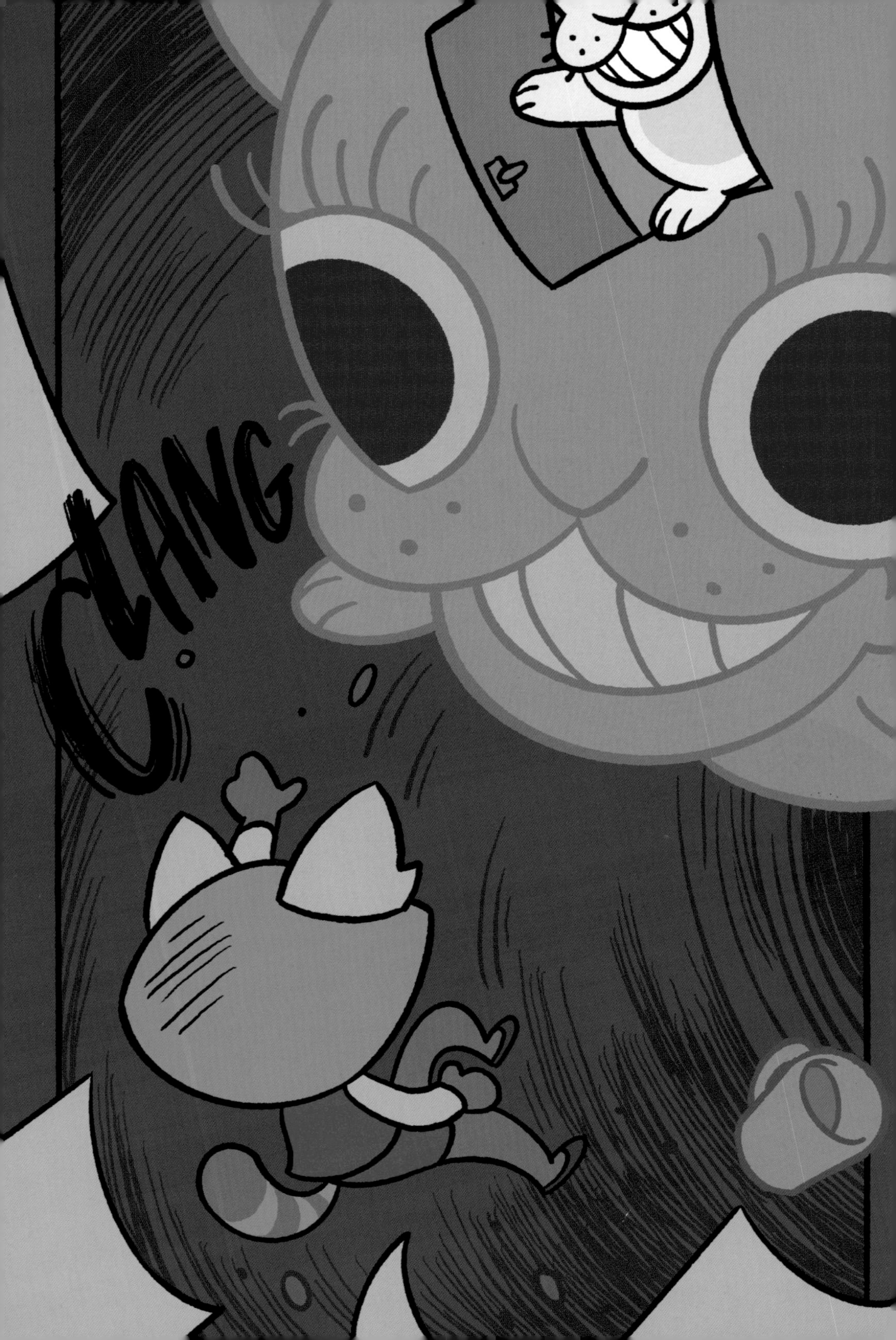
CLANG

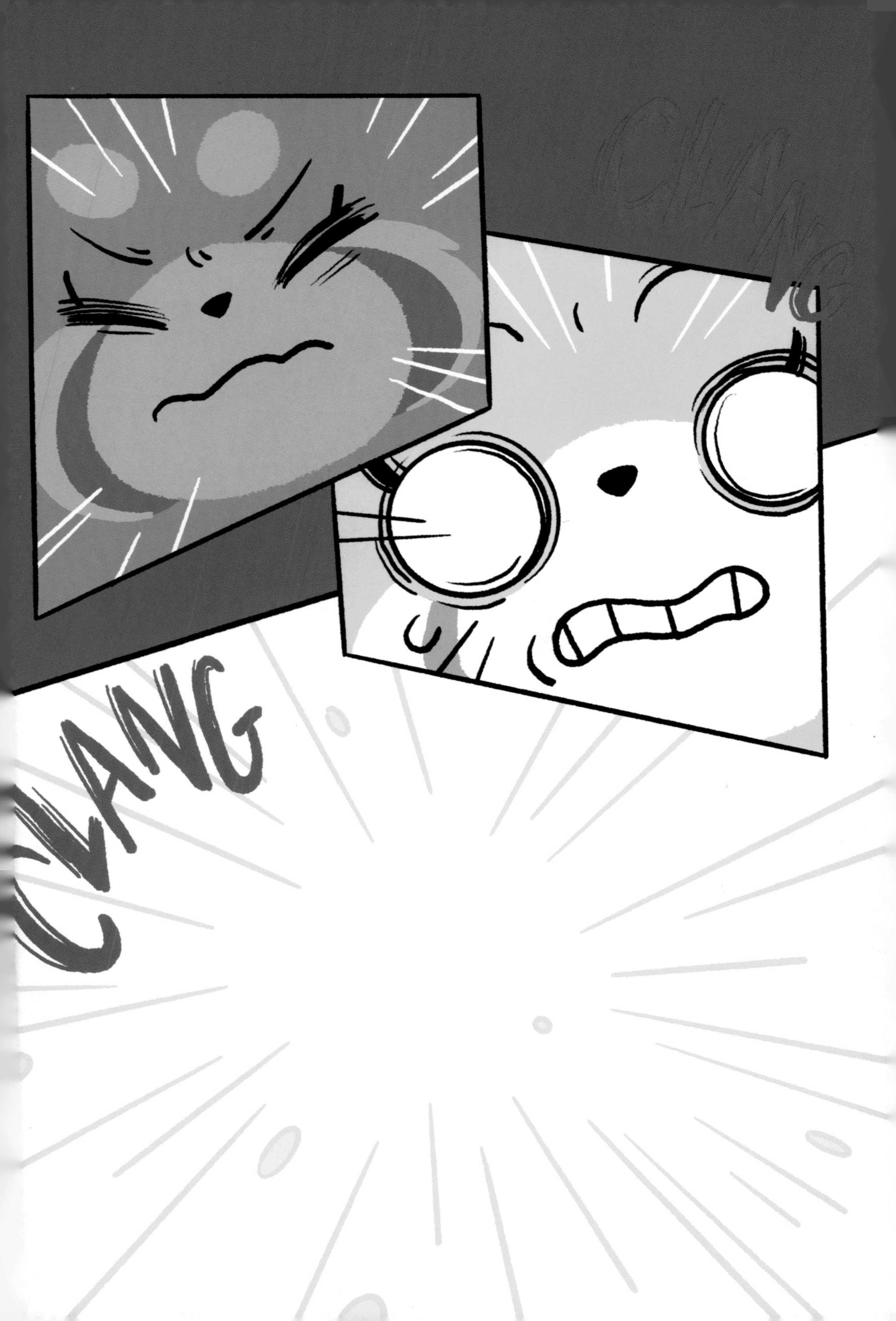
CLANG
CLANG

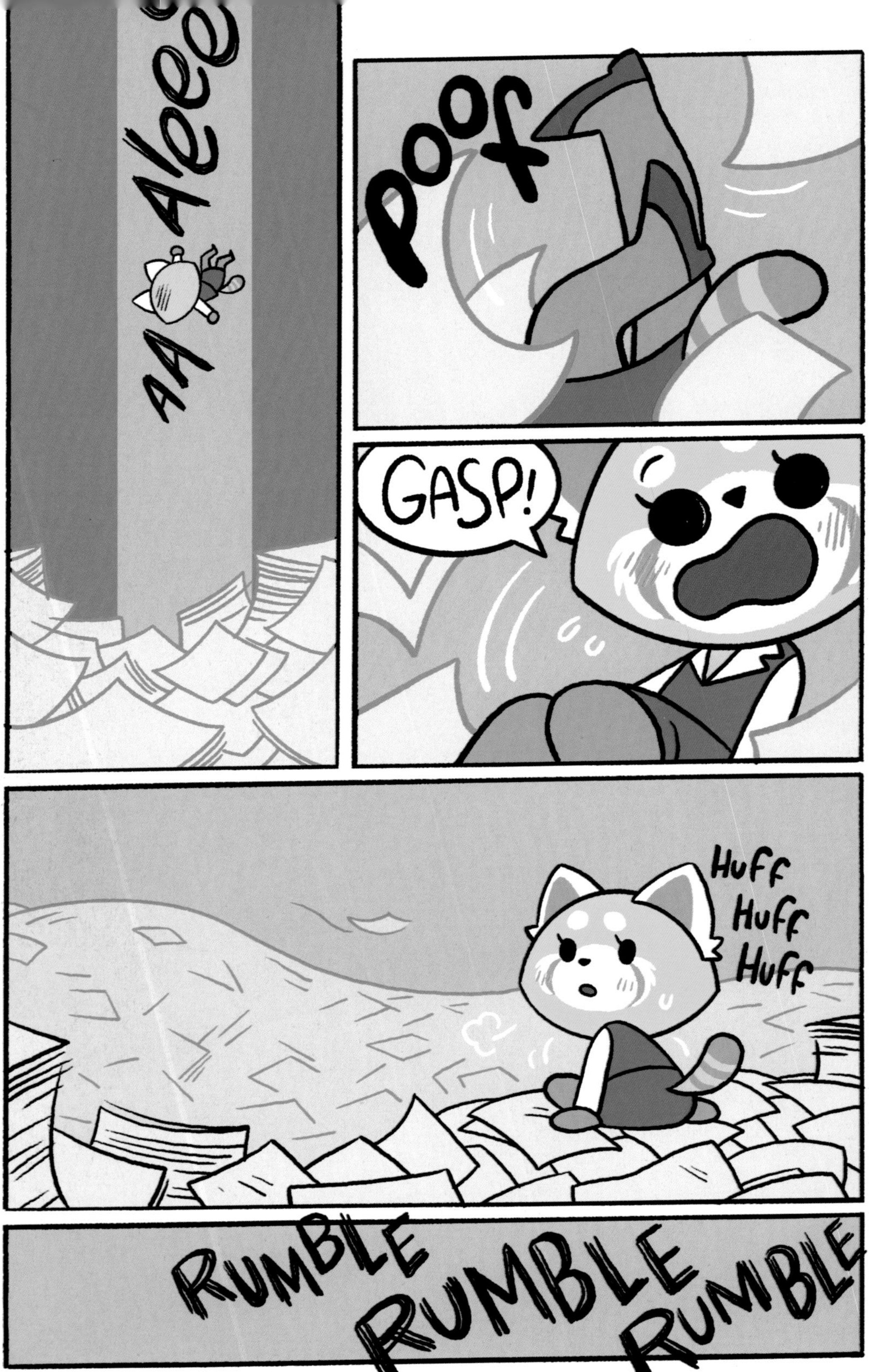
AAAleee
Poof
GASP!
Huff
Huff
Huff
RUMBLE
RUMBLE
RUMBLE

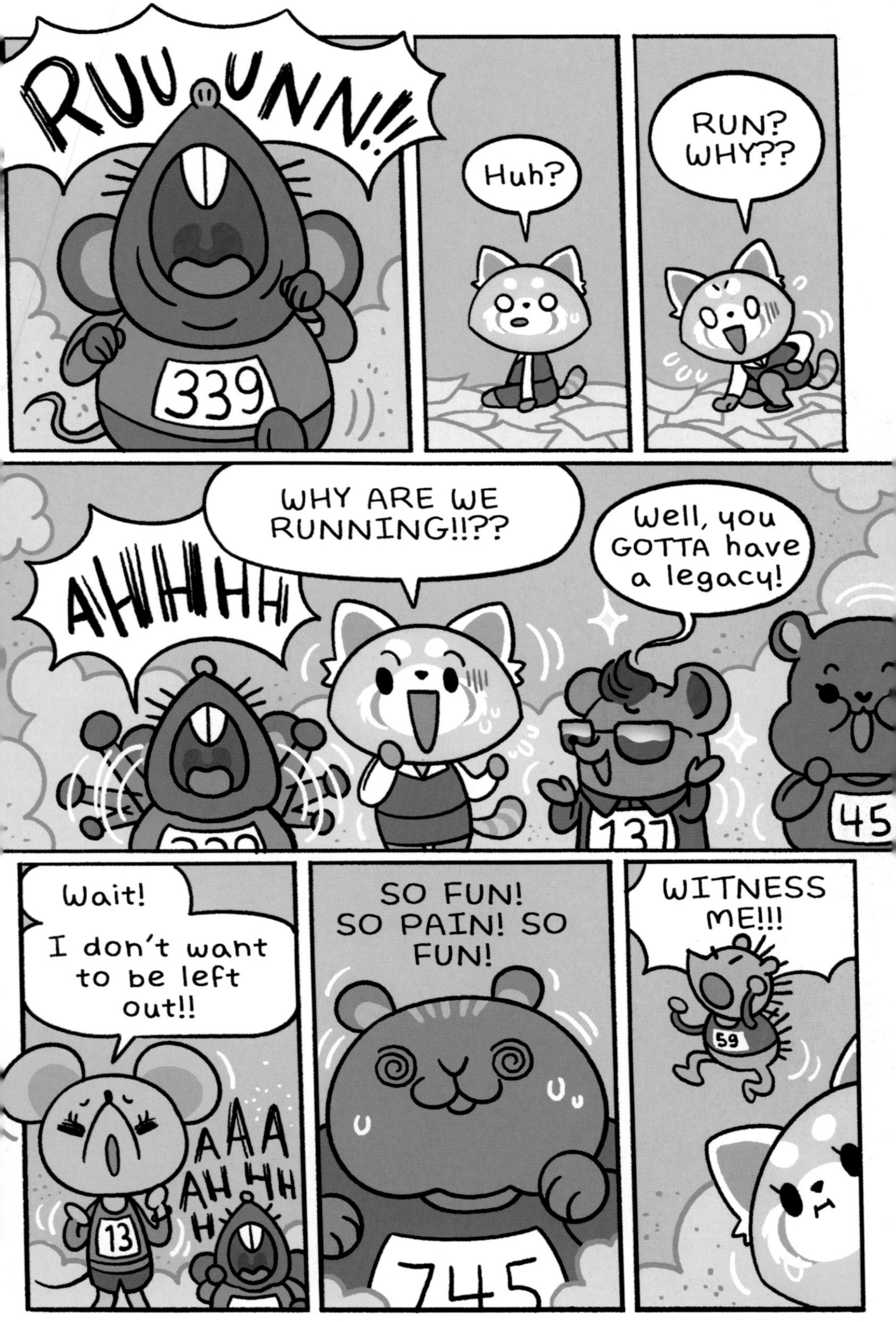
RUUUNN!!!
339
Huh?
RUN? WHY??
AHHHHH
WHY ARE WE RUNNING!!??
Well, you GOTTA have a legacy!
137
45
Wait!
I don't want to be left out!!
13
AAAAHHHH
SO FUN! SO PAIN! SO FUN!
745
WITNESS ME!!!
59

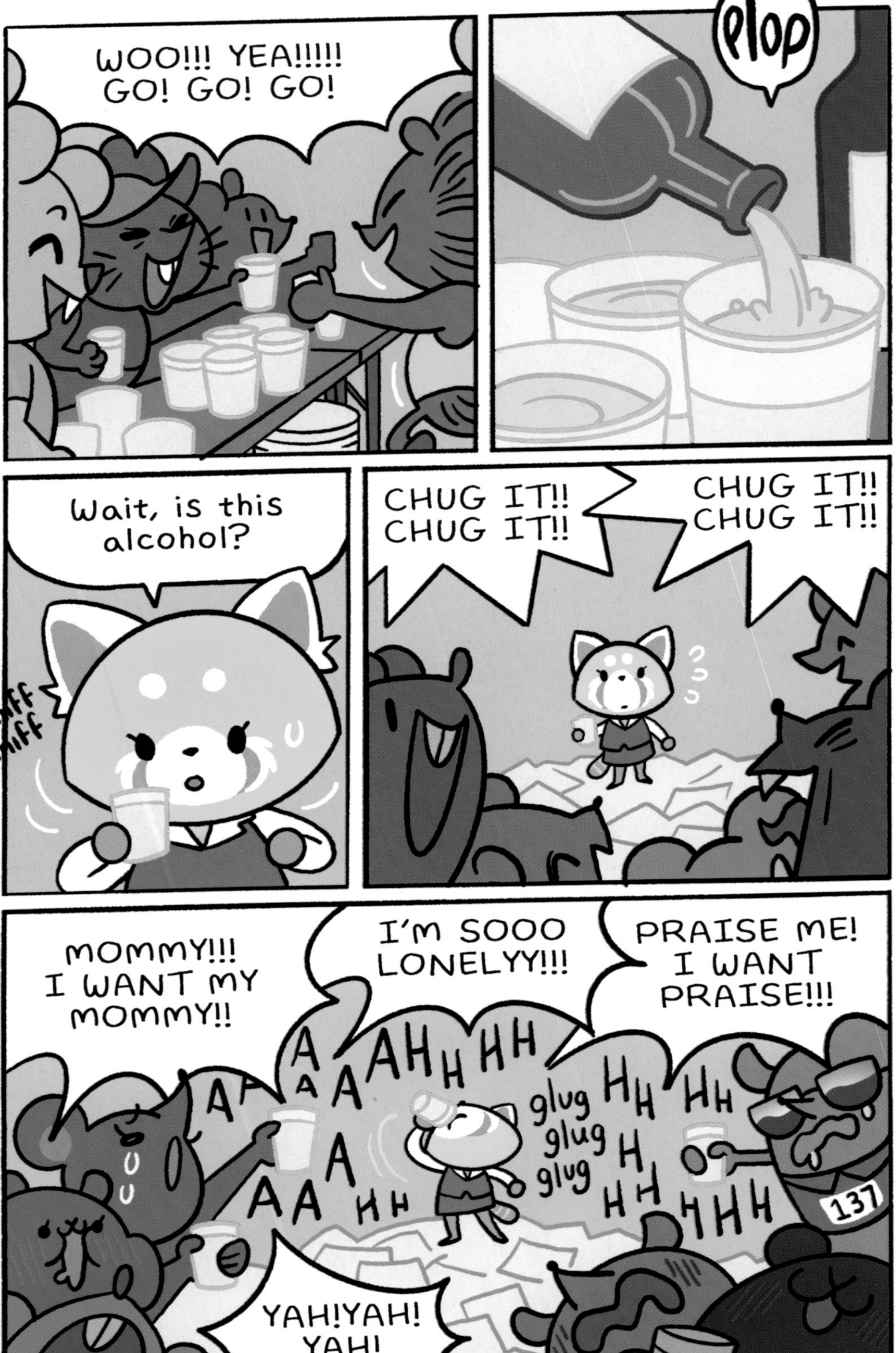

WOO!!! YEA!!!!!
GO! GO! GO!
PLOP
Wait, is this alcohol?
Sniff sniff
CHUG IT!! CHUG IT!!
CHUG IT!! CHUG IT!!
MOMMY!!! I WANT MY MOMMY!!
I'M SOOO LONELYY!!!
PRAISE ME! I WANT PRAISE!!!
AAAAAHHHHH
glug glug glug
YAH!YAH! YAH!
137

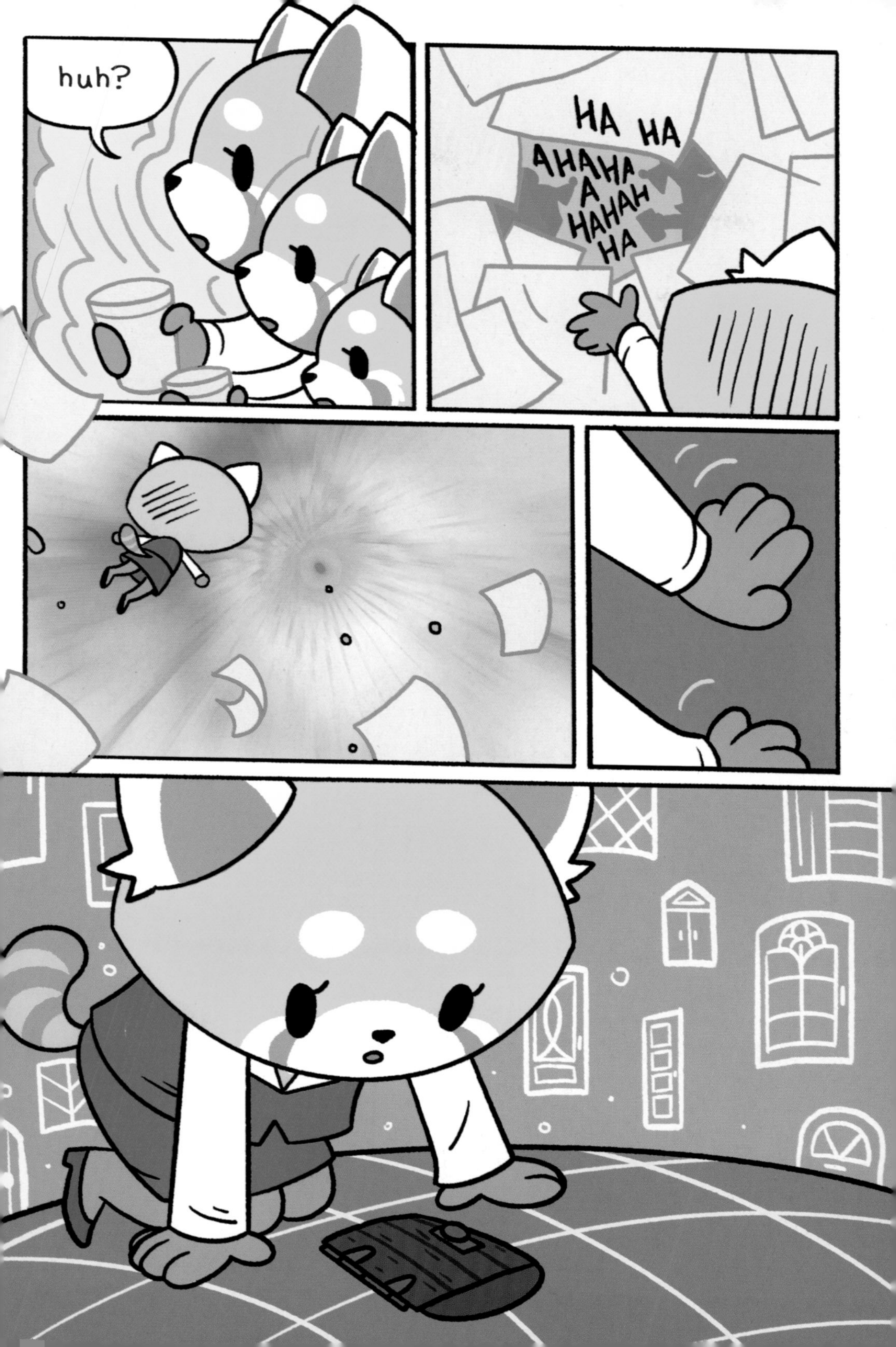
huh?
HA HA
AHAHA
A
HAHAH
HA

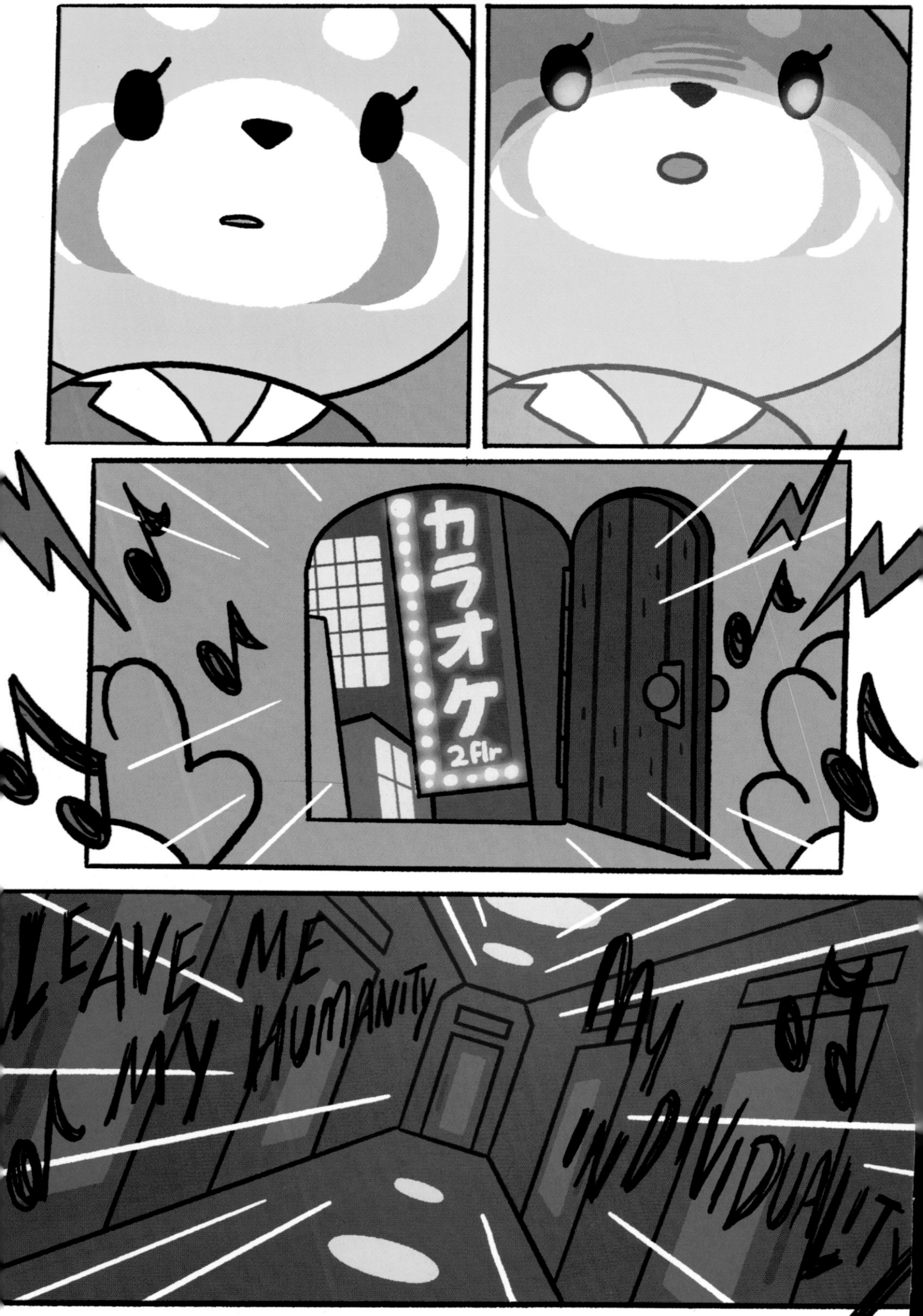
カラオケ
2 Flr
LEAVE ME
MY HUMANITY
My
INDIVIDUALITY

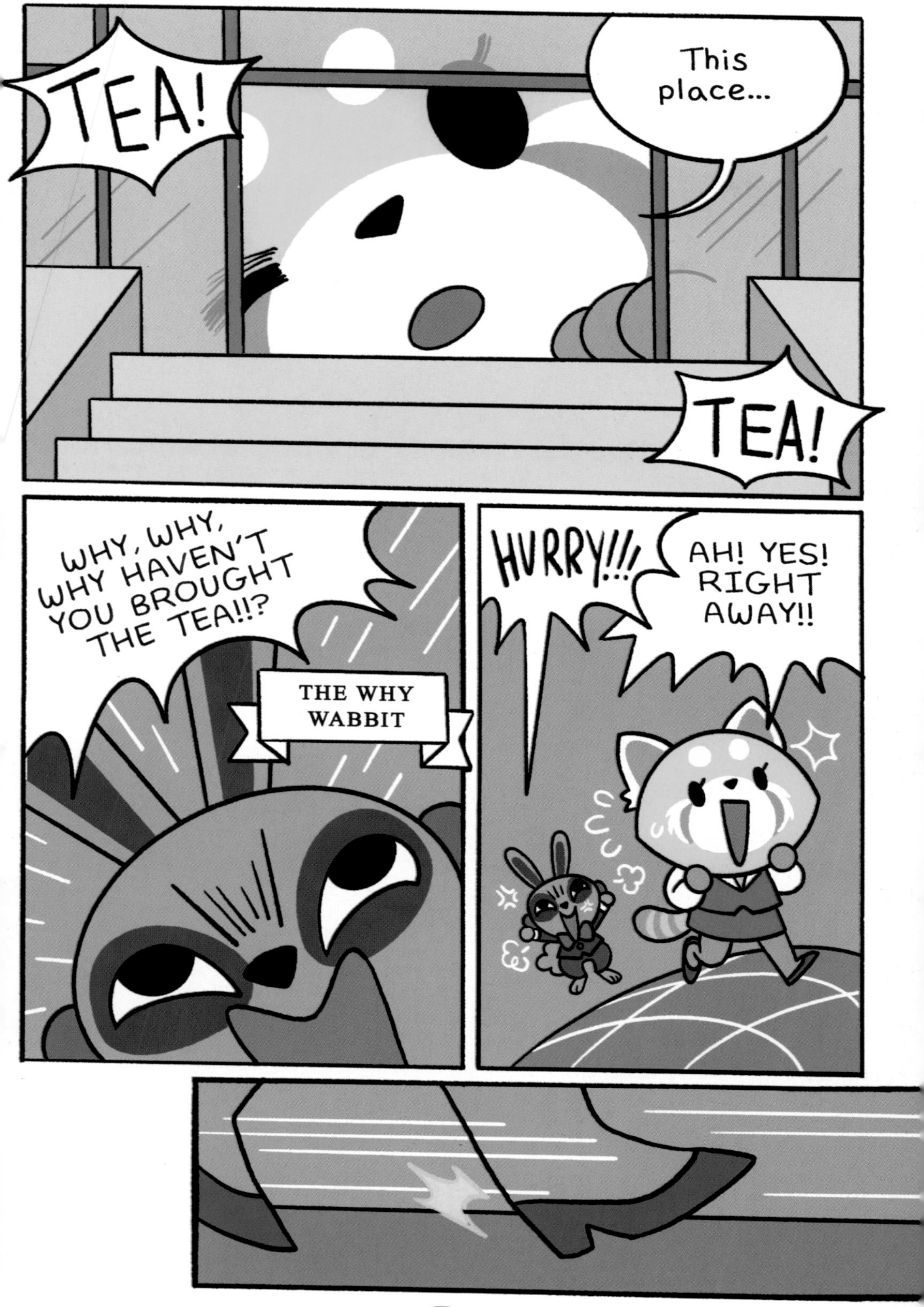
TEA!
This place...
TEA!
WHY, WHY, WHY HAVEN'T YOU BROUGHT THE TEA!!?
THE WHY WABBIT
HURRY!!!
AH! YES! RIGHT AWAY!!

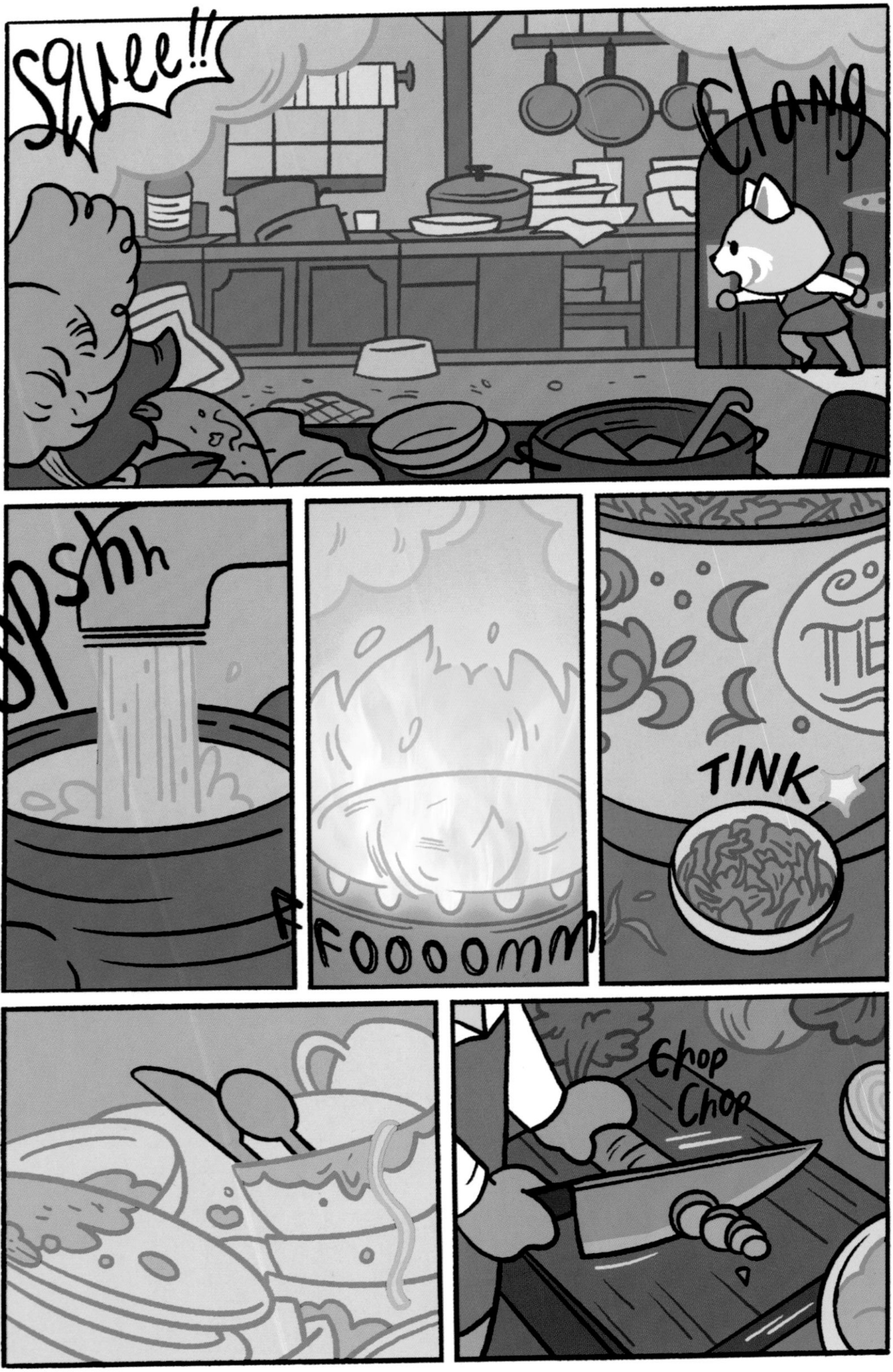
SQUEE!!
Clang
Spshh
RFOOOOMM
TINK
Chop
Chop

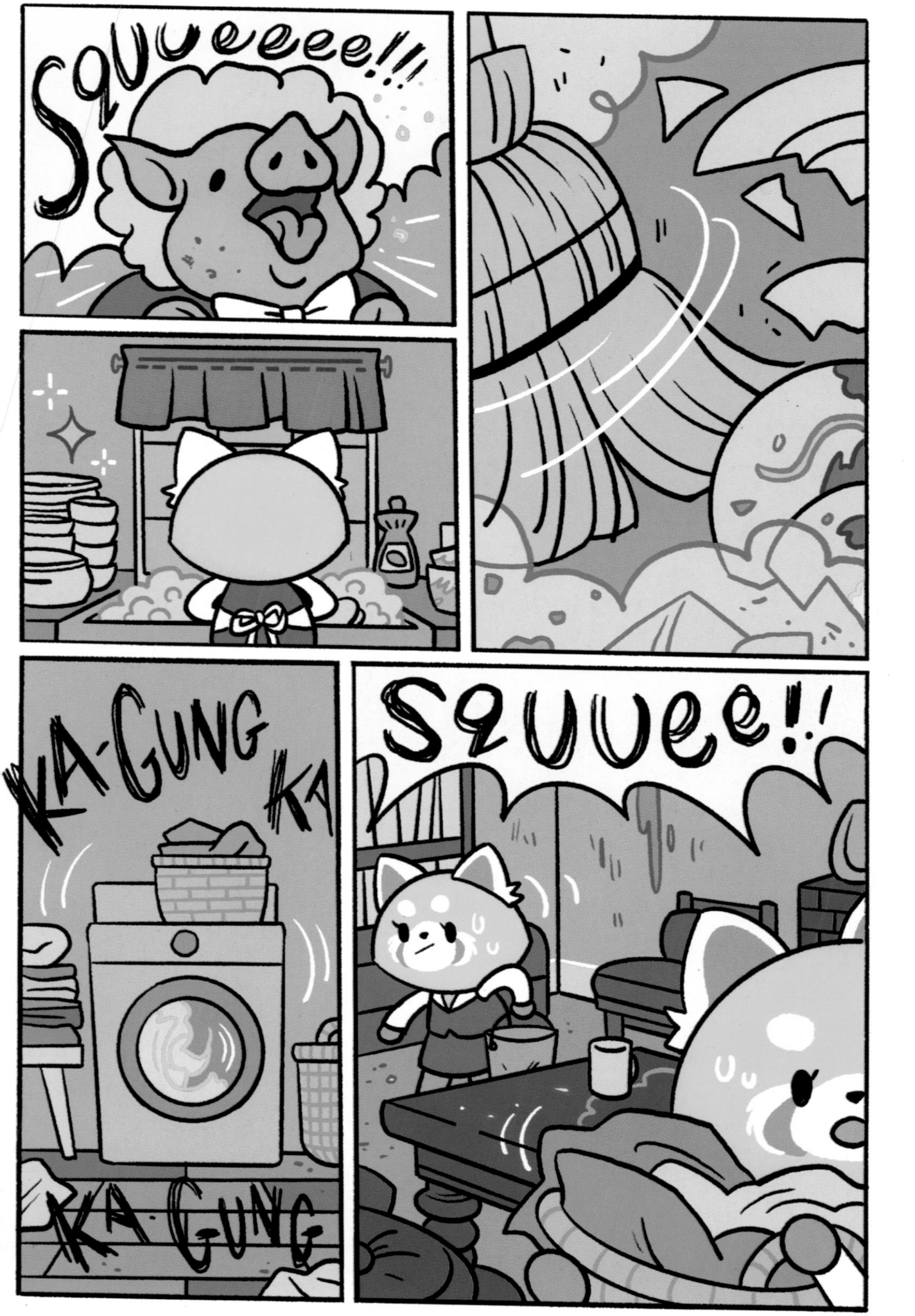
SQUEEEEE!!!
KA-GUNG KA
KA-GUNG
SQUEE!!

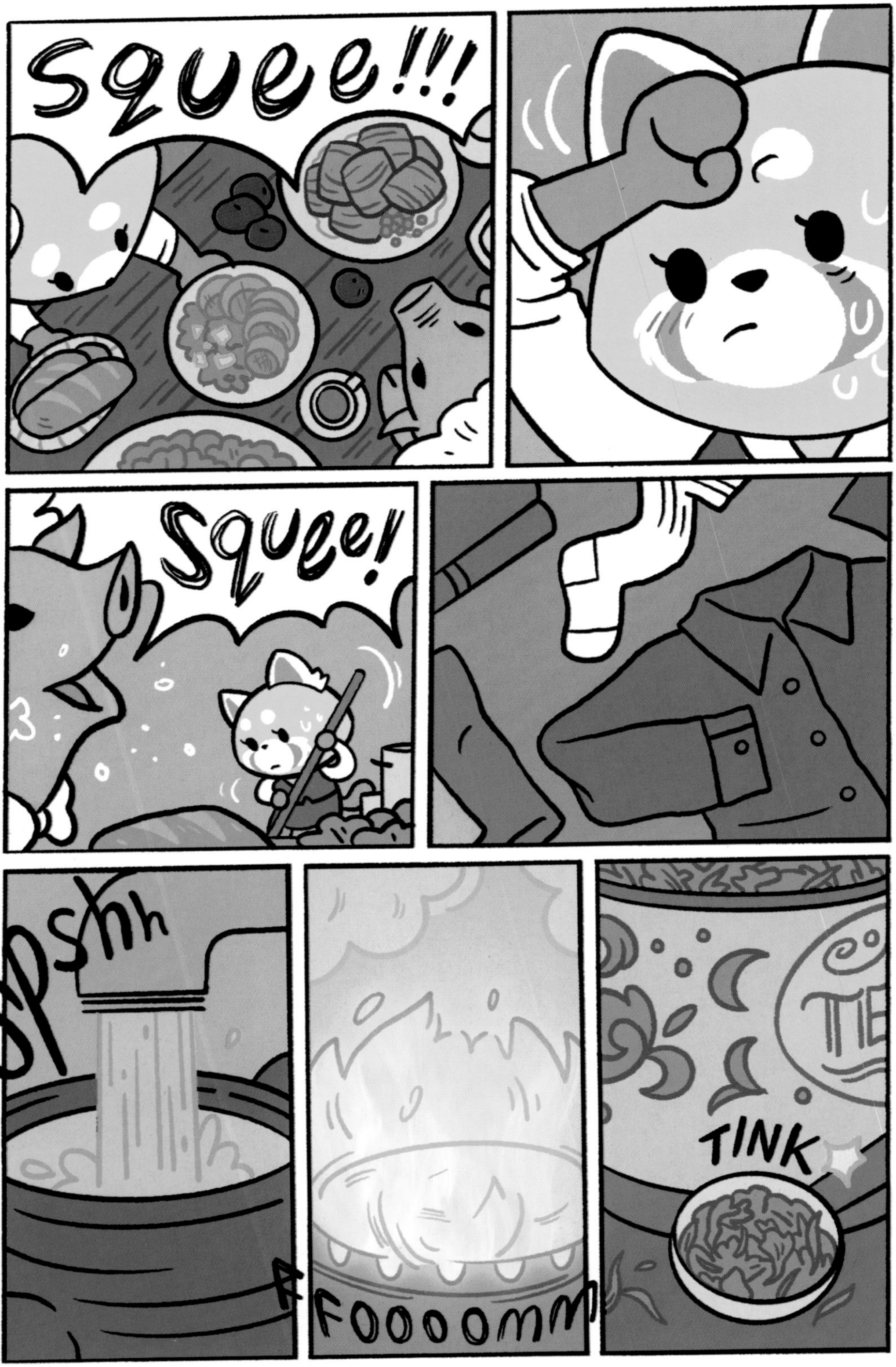
SQUEE!!!
SQUEE!
SPSHH
FFOOOOMM
TINK

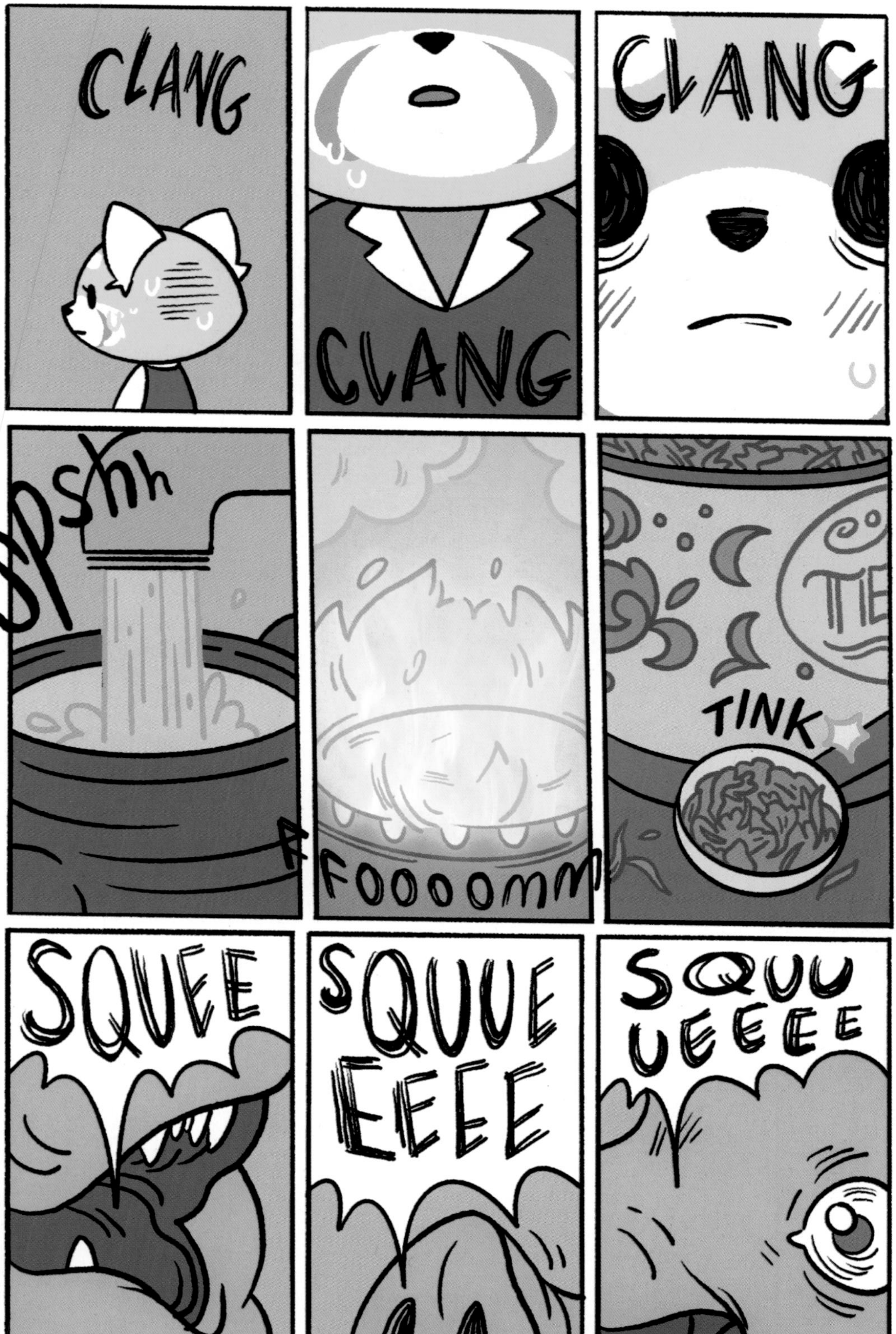
CLANG
CLANG
CLANG
Spshh
FFOOOOMM
TINK
SQUEE
SQUUE EEEE
SQUU UEEEE

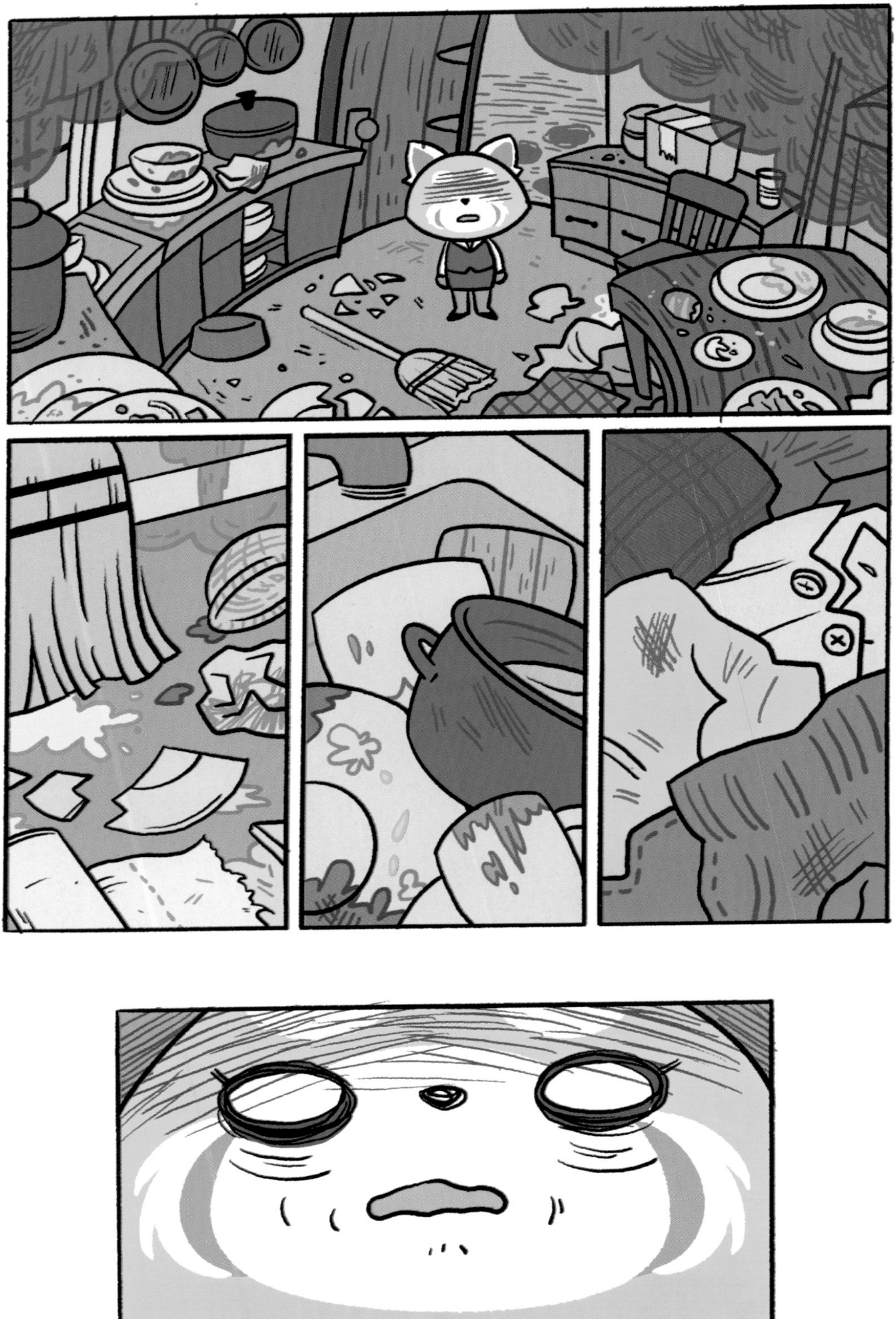

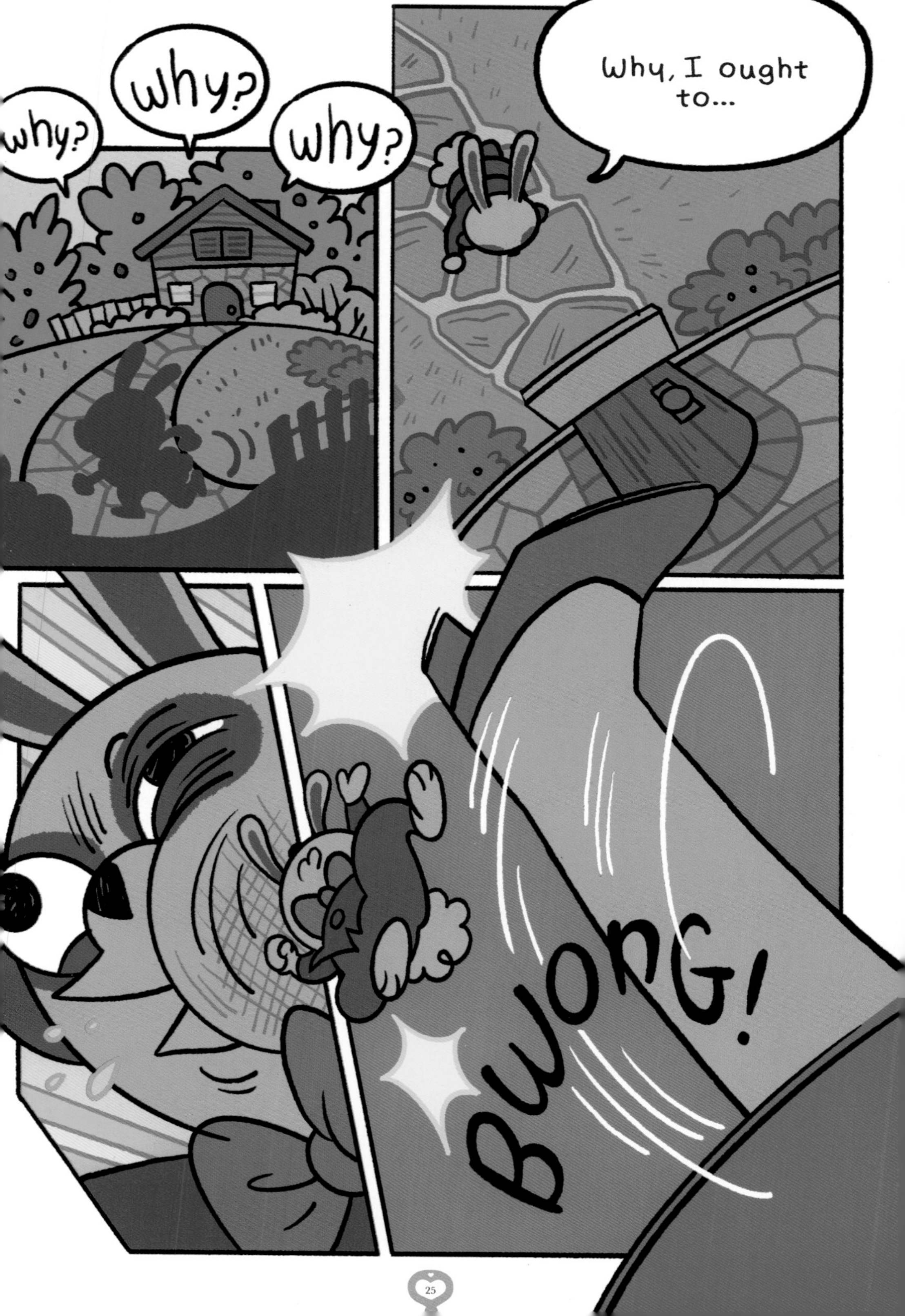
why?
why?
why?
Why, I ought to...
BWONG!

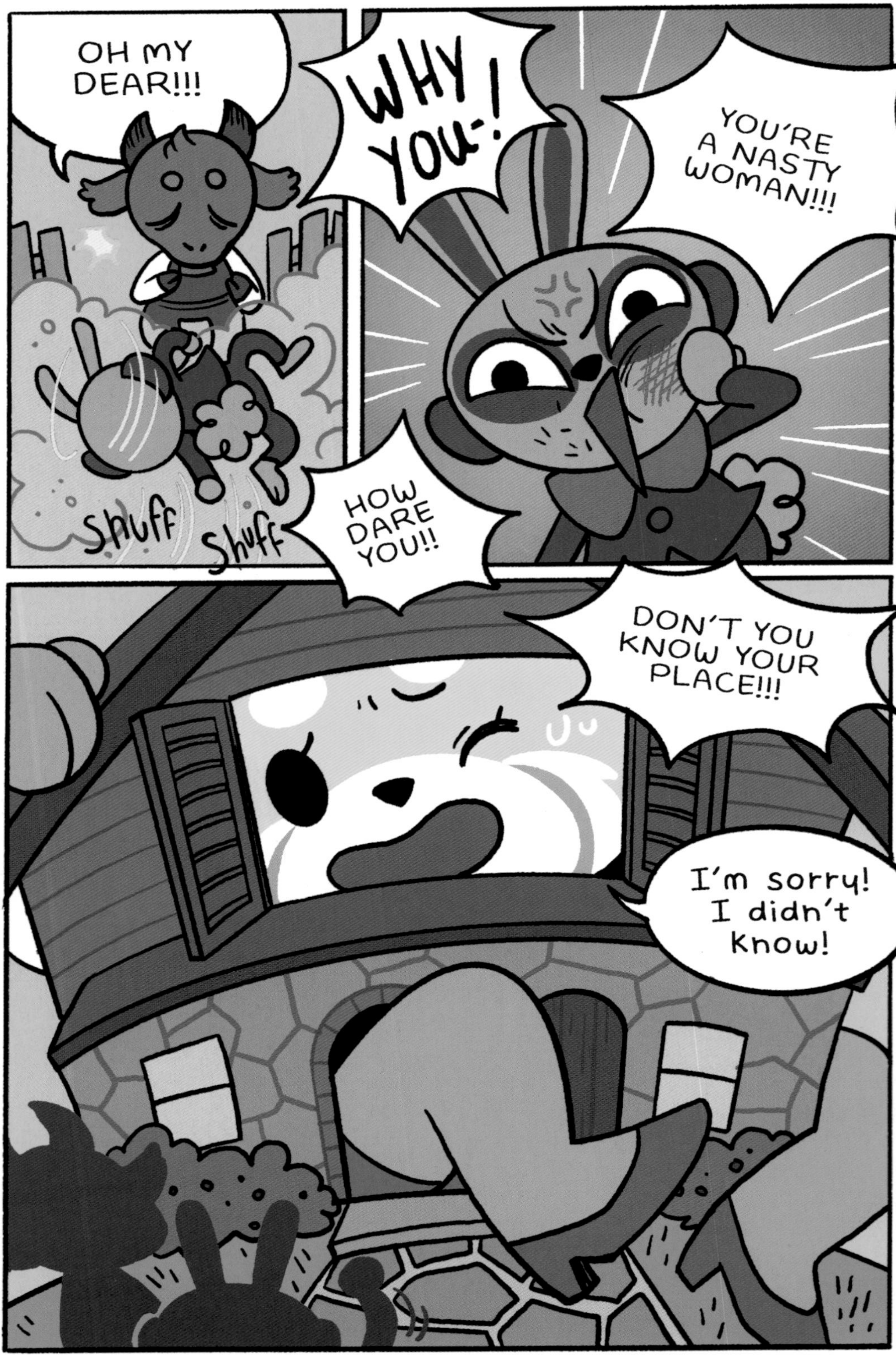
OH MY DEAR!!!
Shuff Shuff
WHY YOU-!
YOU'RE A NASTY WOMAN!!!
HOW DARE YOU!!
DON'T YOU KNOW YOUR PLACE!!!
I'm sorry! I didn't know!

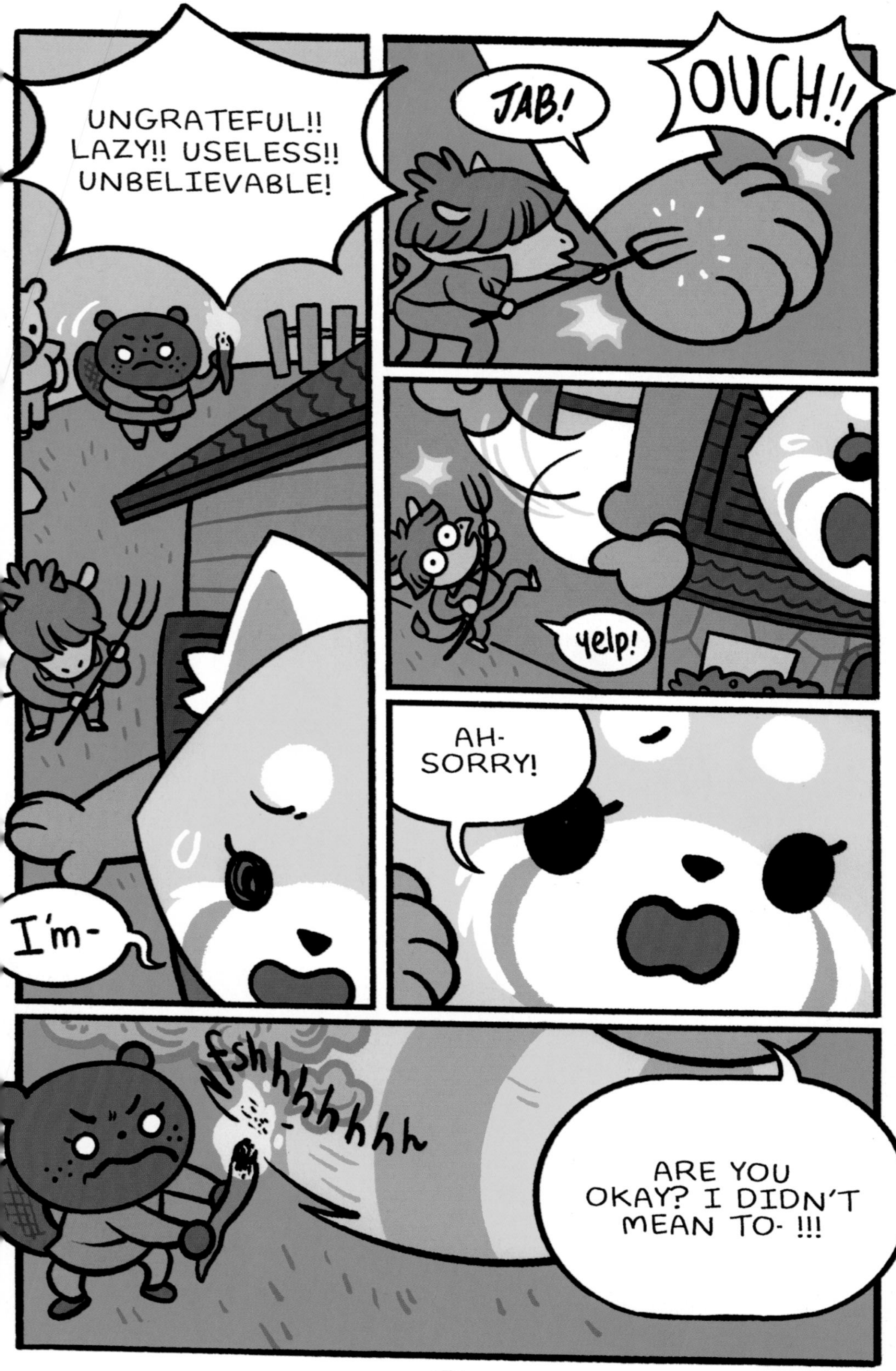
UNGRATEFUL!! LAZY!! USELESS!! UNBELIEVABLE!
JAB!
OUCH!!
yelp!
I'm-
AH- SORRY!
fshhhhhhhh
ARE YOU OKAY? I DIDN'T MEAN TO- !!!

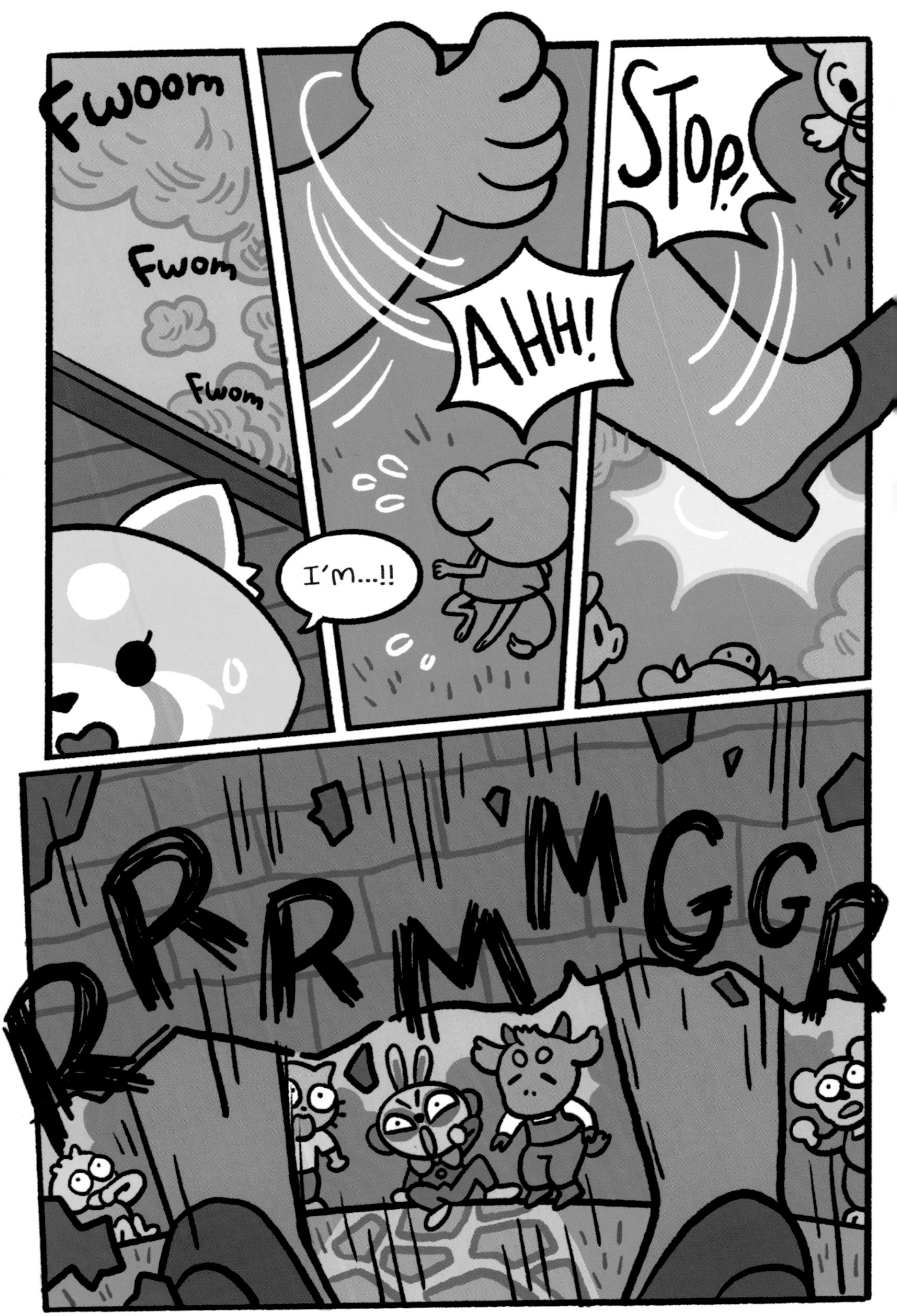
Fwoom
Fwom
Fwom
I'm...!!
AHH!
STOP!
RRRRMMGGR

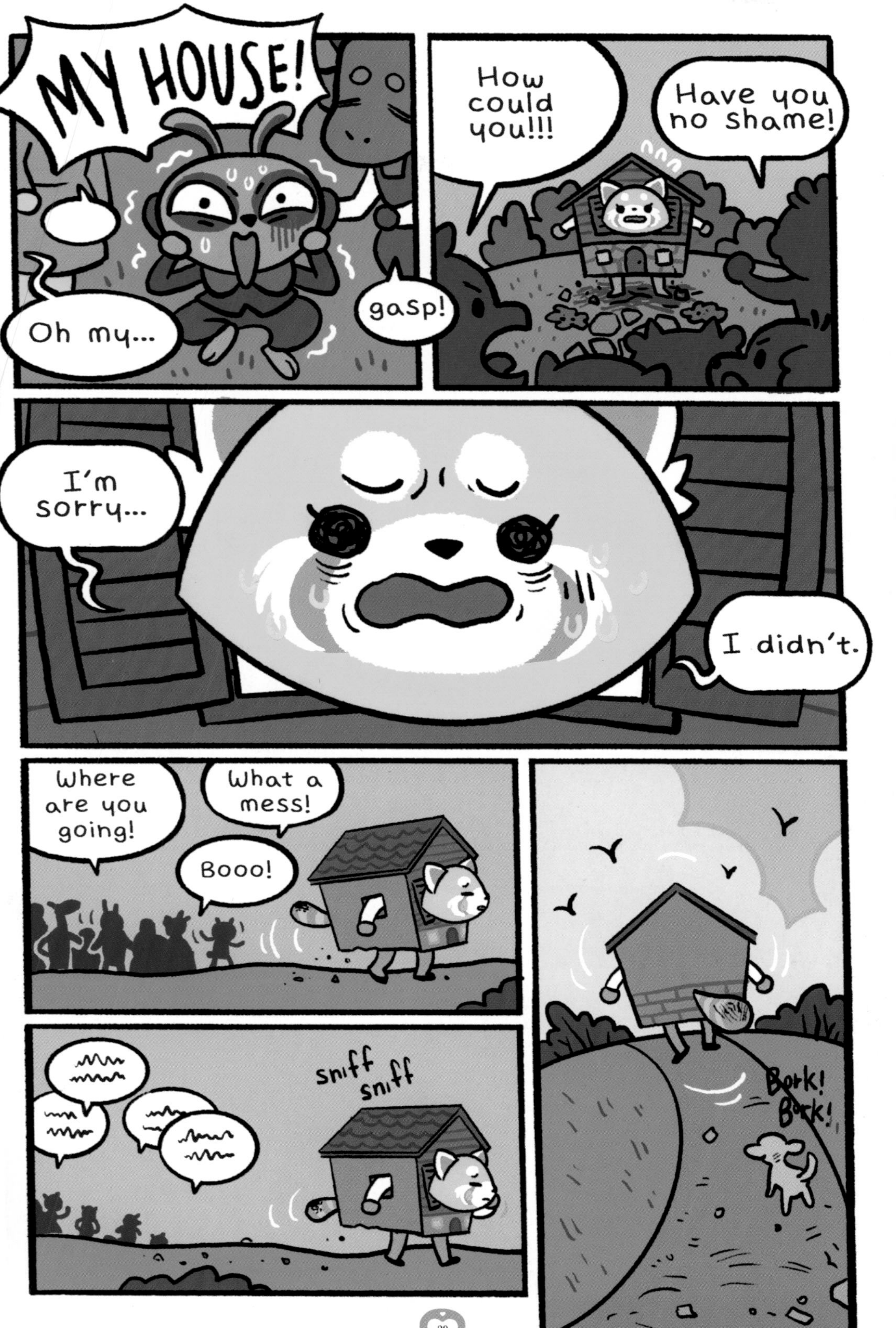
MY HOUSE!
Oh my...
gasp!
How could you!!!
Have you no shame!
I'm sorry...
I didn't.
Where are you going!
What a mess!
Booo!
sniff sniff
Bork! Bork!

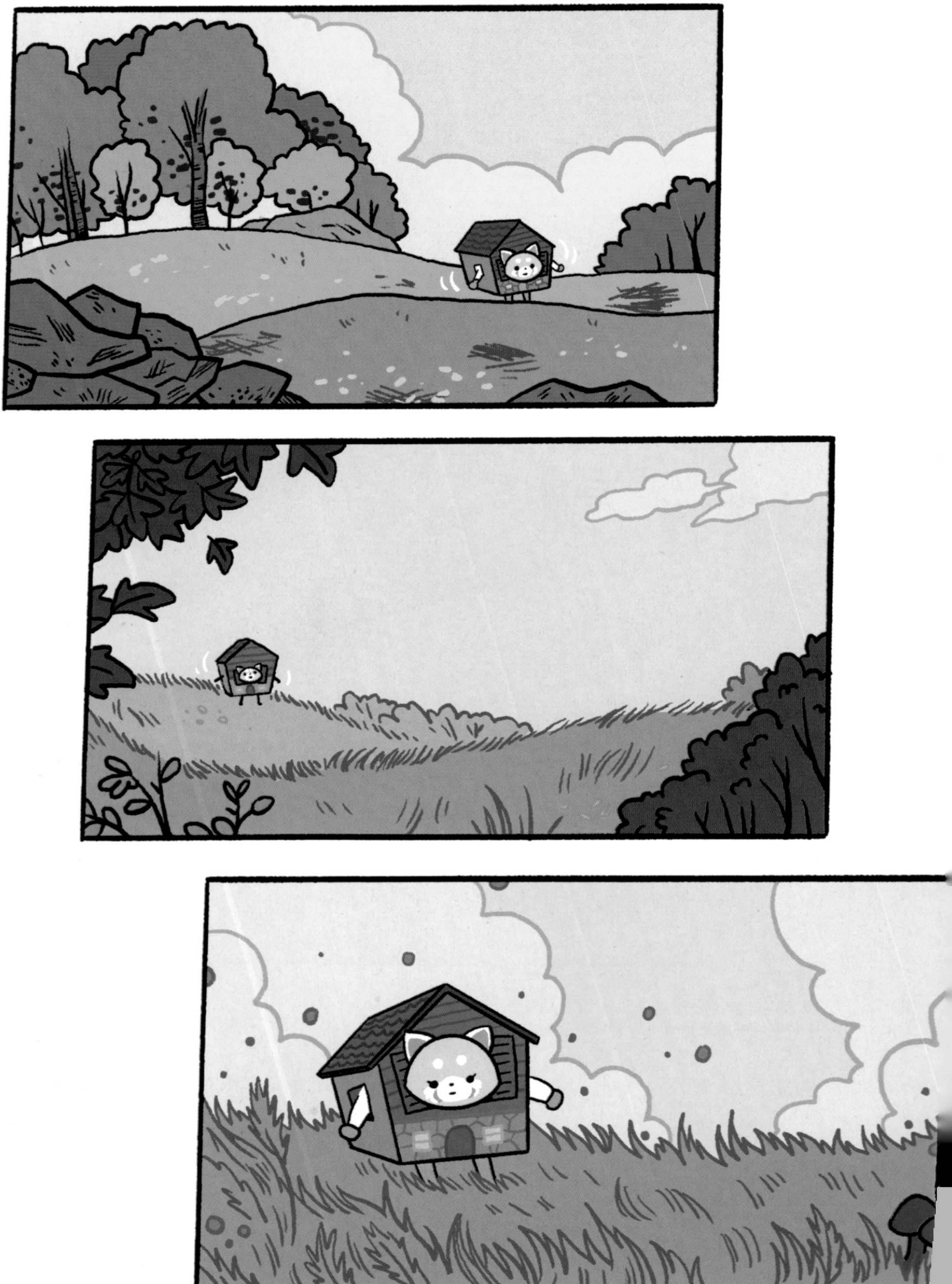

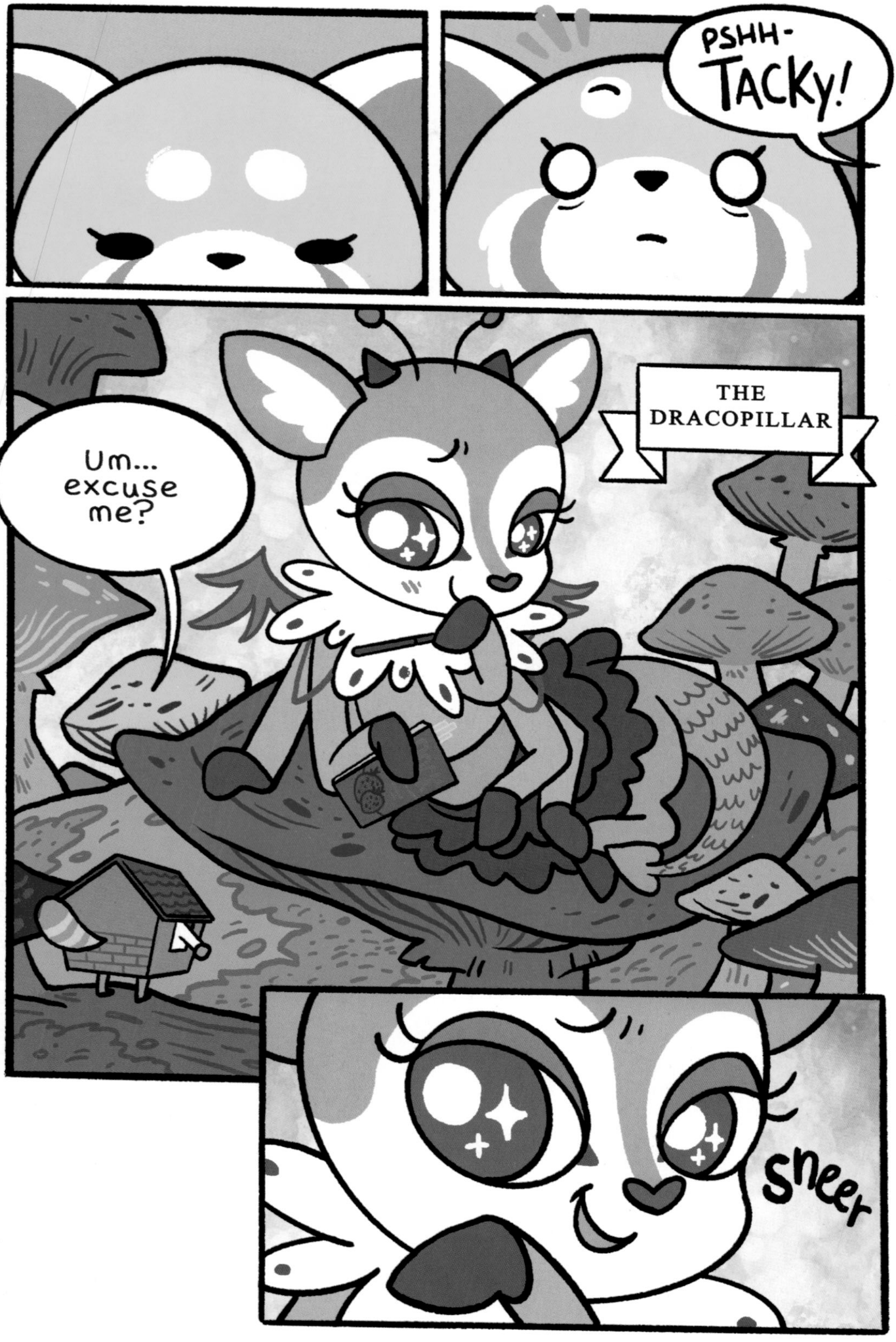
PSHH-TACKY!
THE DRACOPILLAR
Um... excuse me?
sneer

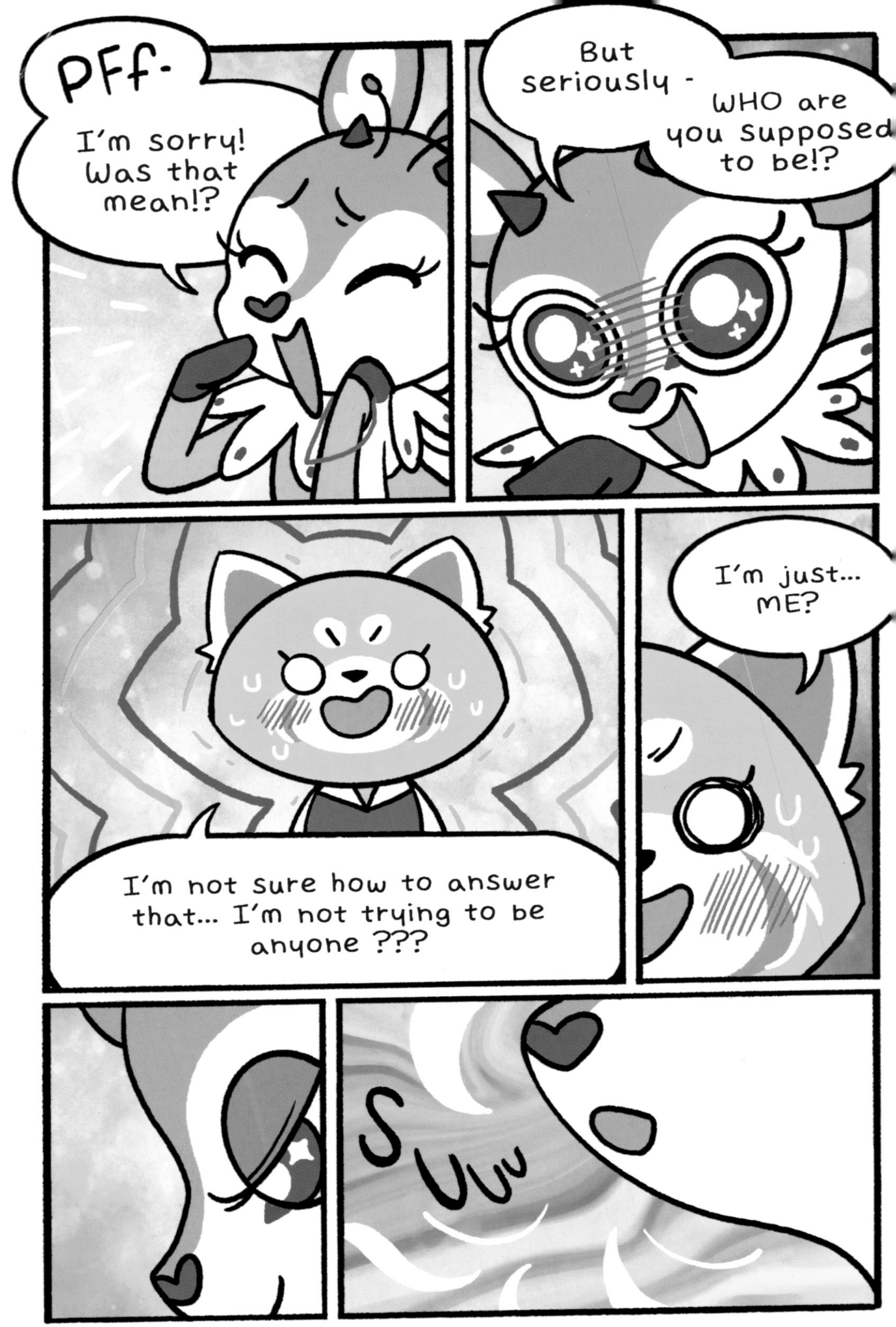
PFf-
I'm sorry! Was that mean!?
But seriously -
WHO are you supposed to be!?
I'm not sure how to answer that... I'm not trying to be anyone ???
I'm just... ME?
S
Uuu

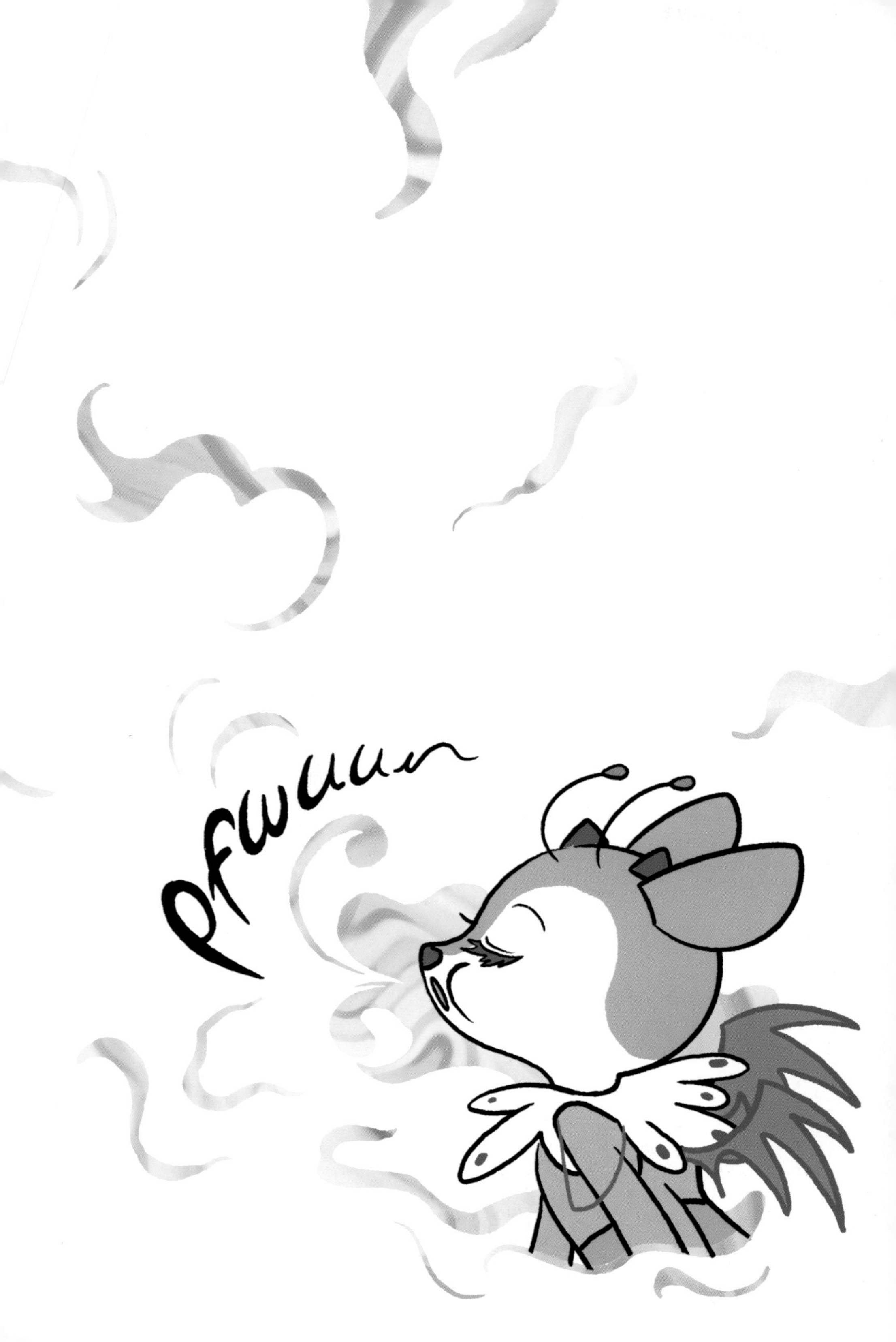
pfwuuu

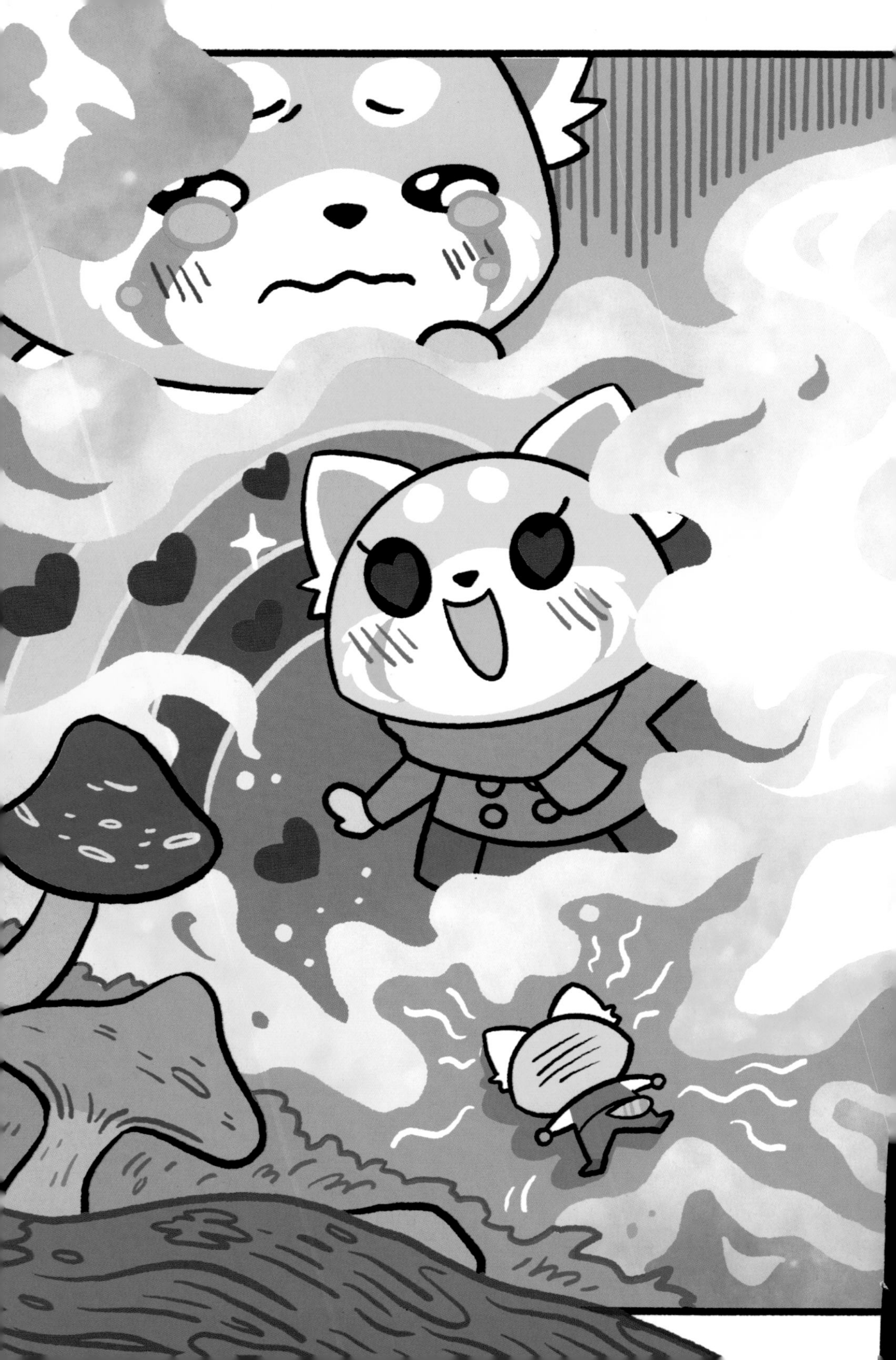

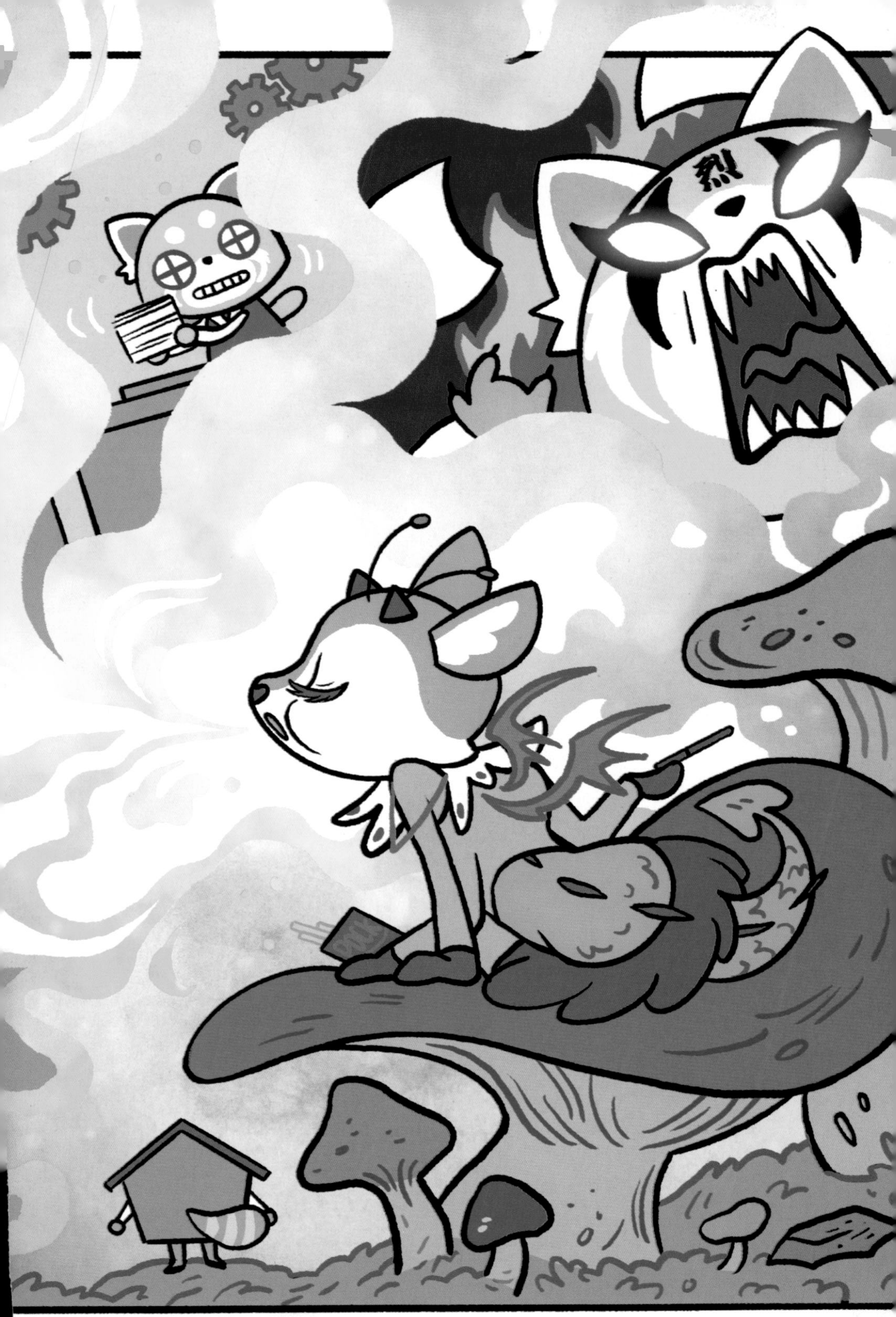
烈

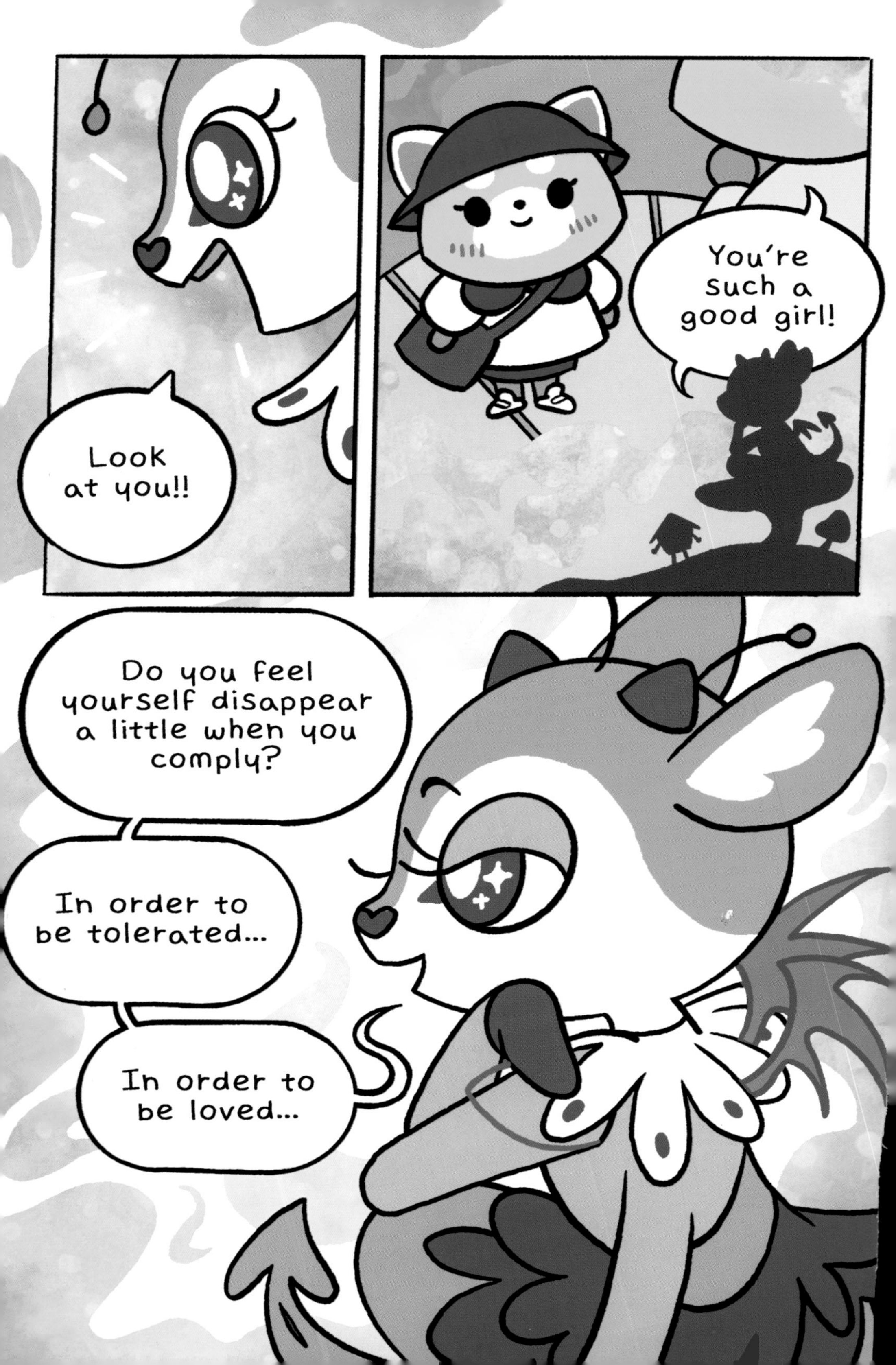
Look at you!!
You're such a good girl!
Do you feel yourself disappear a little when you comply?
In order to be tolerated...
In order to be loved...

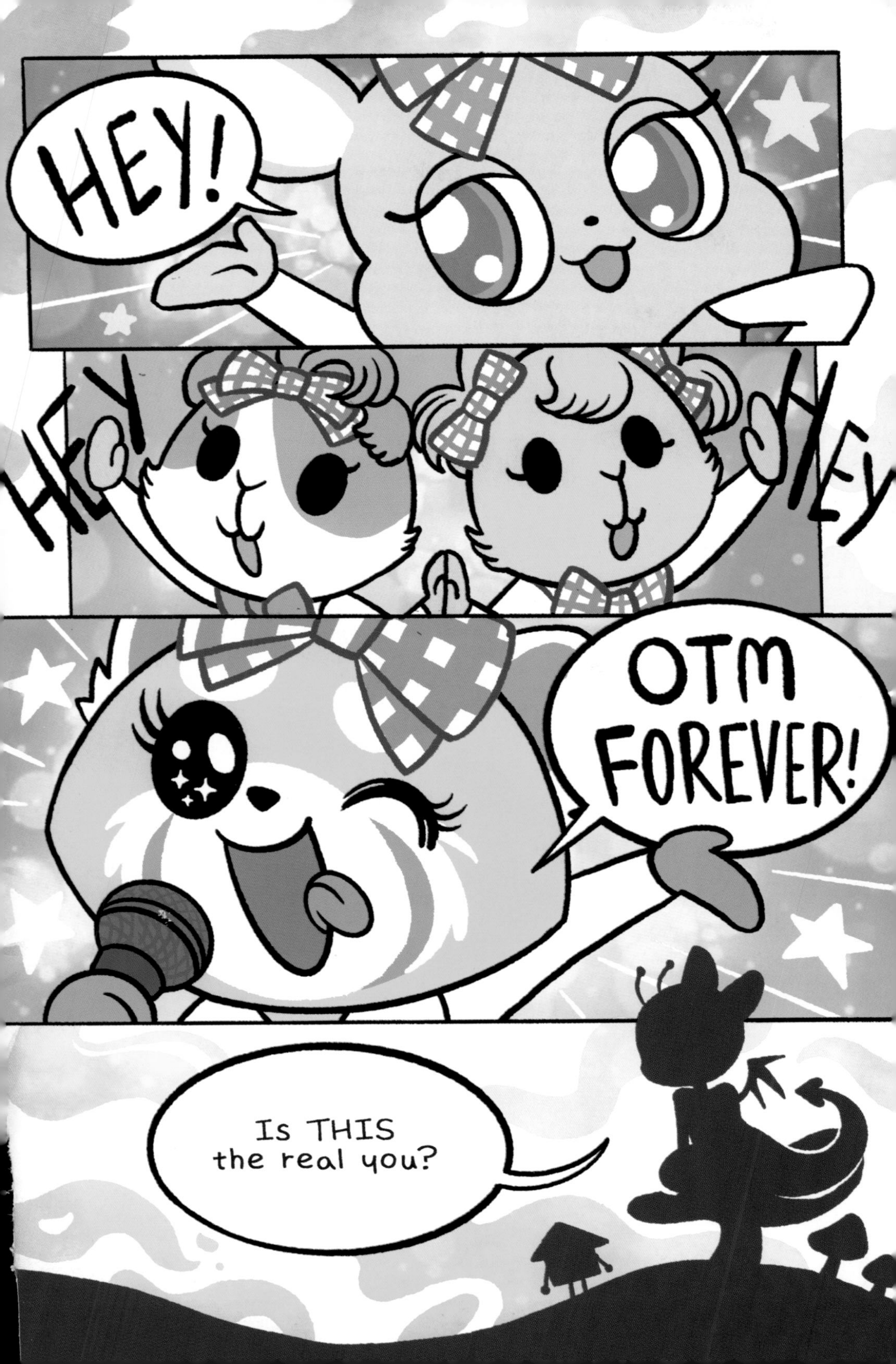
HEY!
HEY!
HEY
OTM FOREVER!
Is THIS the real you?

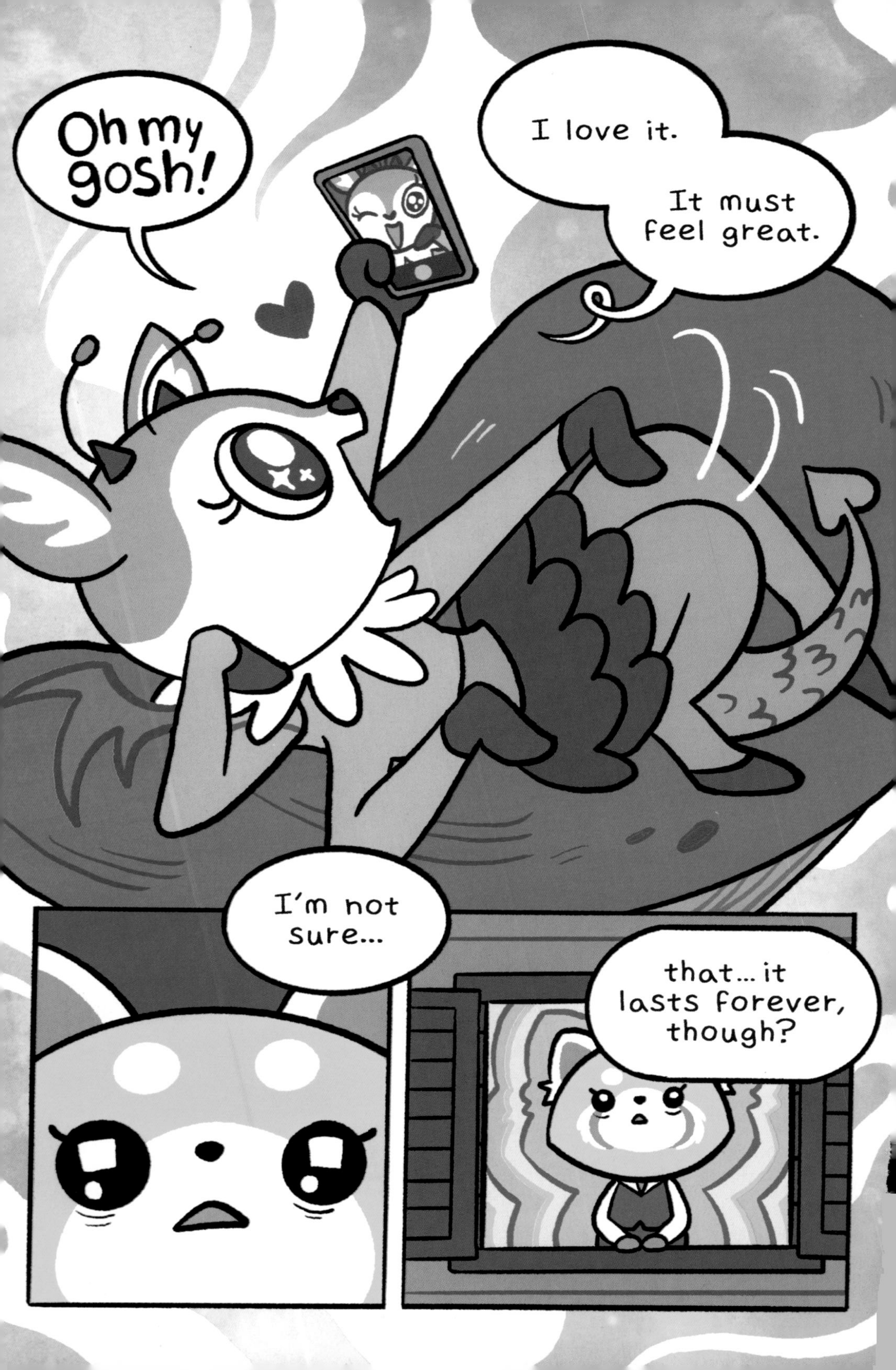
Oh my gosh!
I love it.
It must feel great.
I'm not sure...
that... it lasts forever, though?

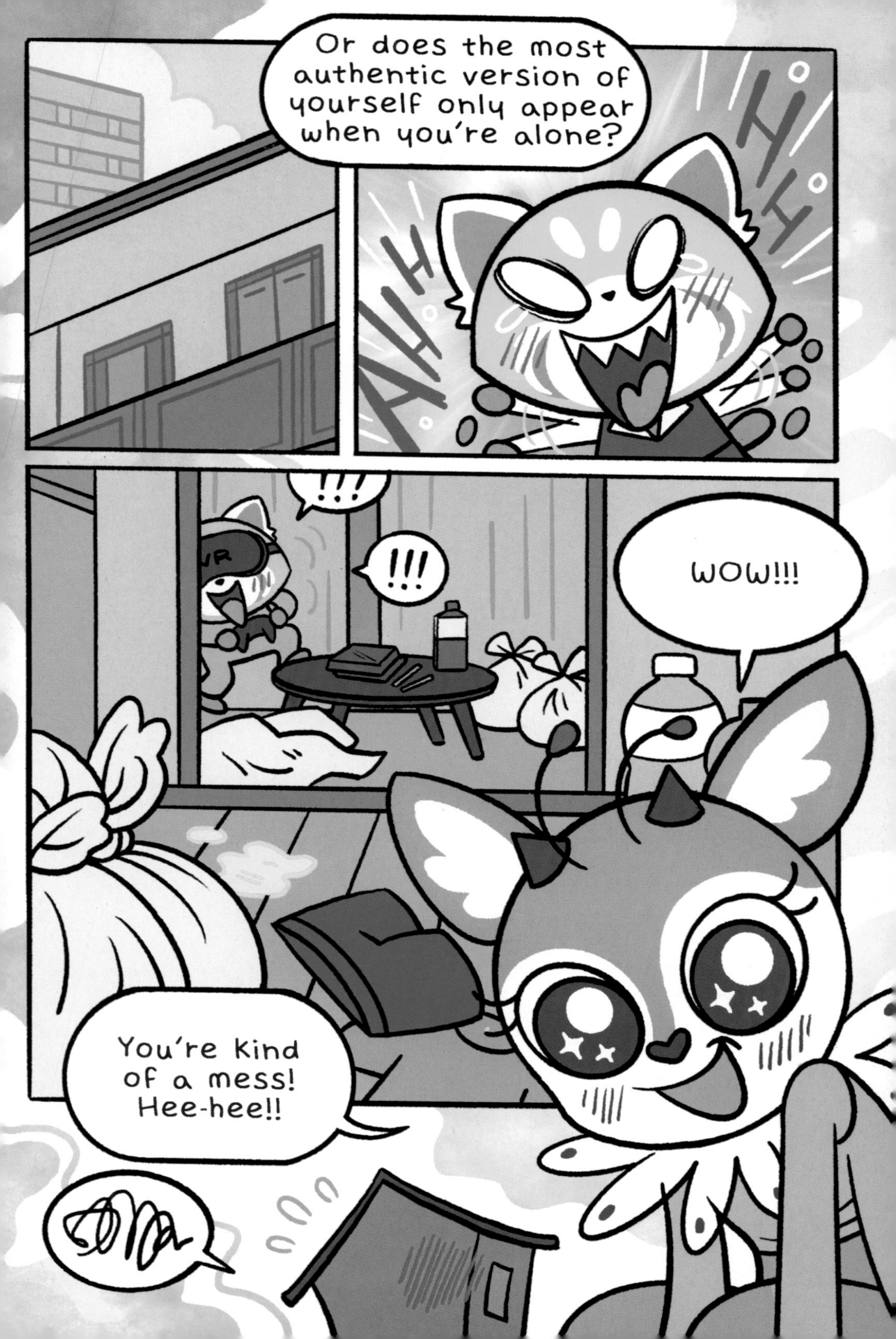
Or does the most authentic version of yourself only appear when you're alone?
AHHHHH
!!!
!!!
WOW!!!
You're kind of a mess! Hee-hee!!

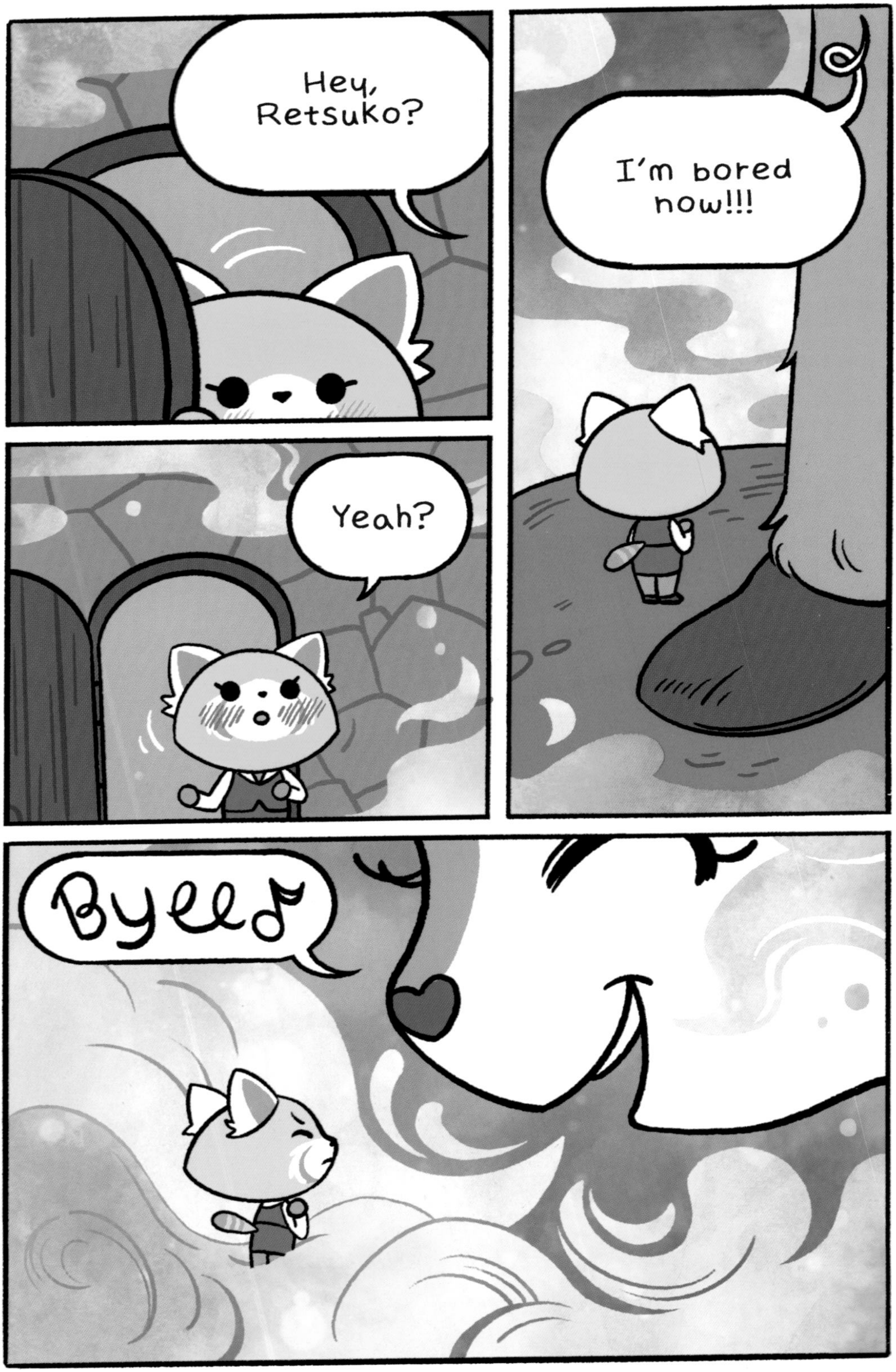
Hey, Retsuko?
I'm bored now!!!
Yeah?
Byeee♪

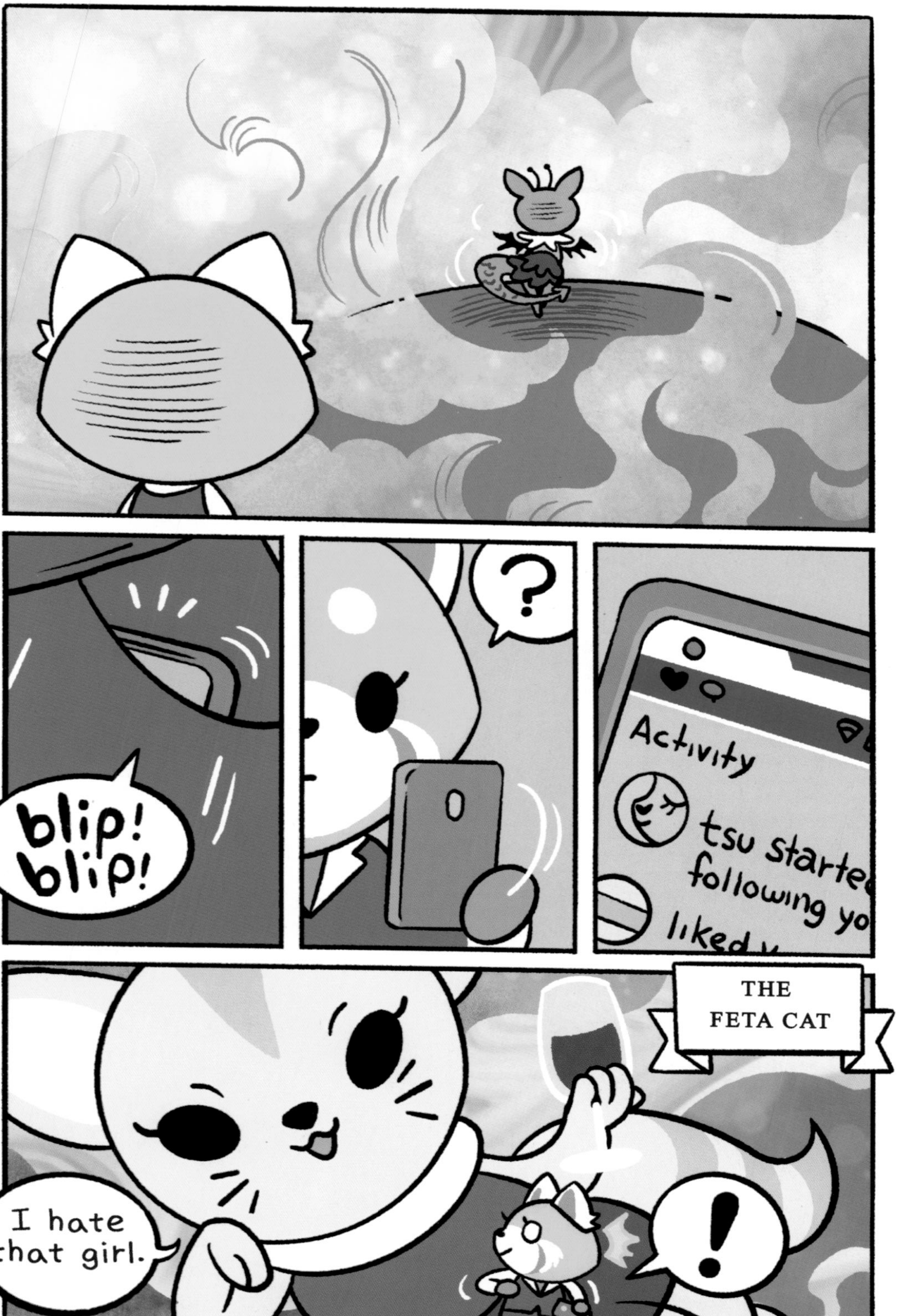
blip! blip!
?
Activity
tsu starte
following yo
liked
THE FETA CAT
I hate that girl.
!

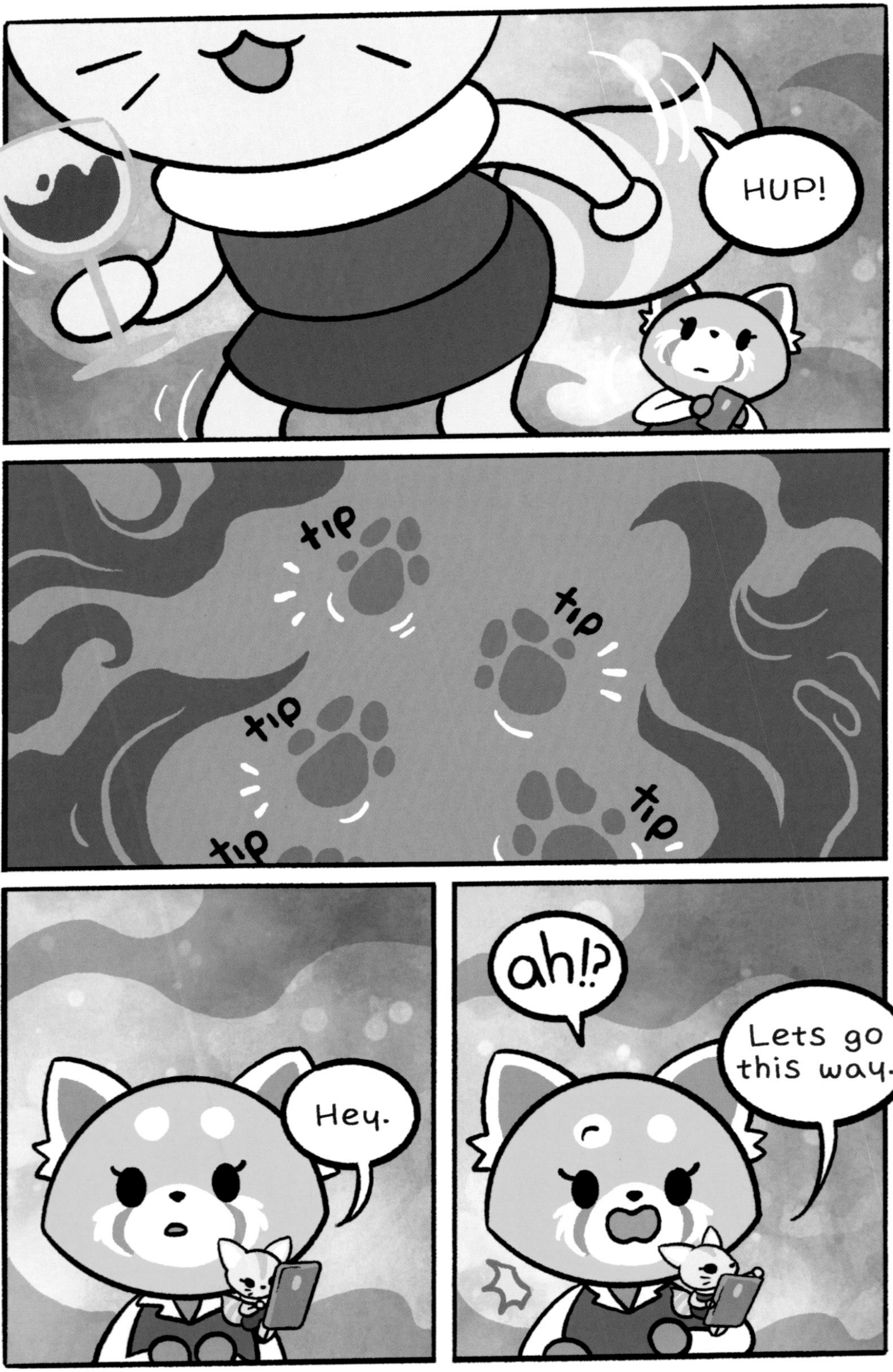
HUP!
tip
tip
tip
tip
tip
Hey.
ah!?
Lets go this way.

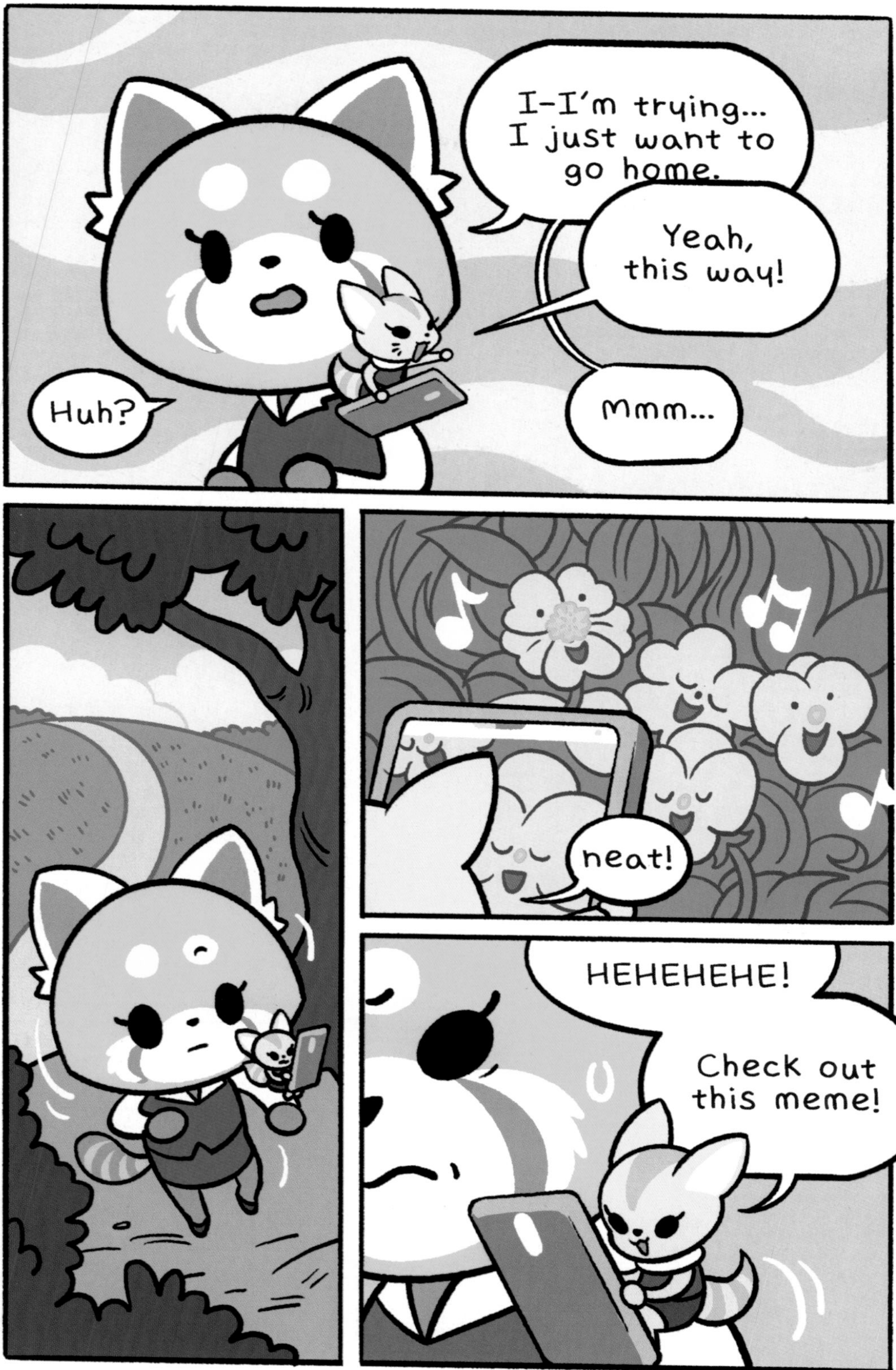
I-I'm trying... I just want to go home.
Yeah, this way!
Huh?
Mmm...
neat!
HEHEHEHE!
Check out this meme!

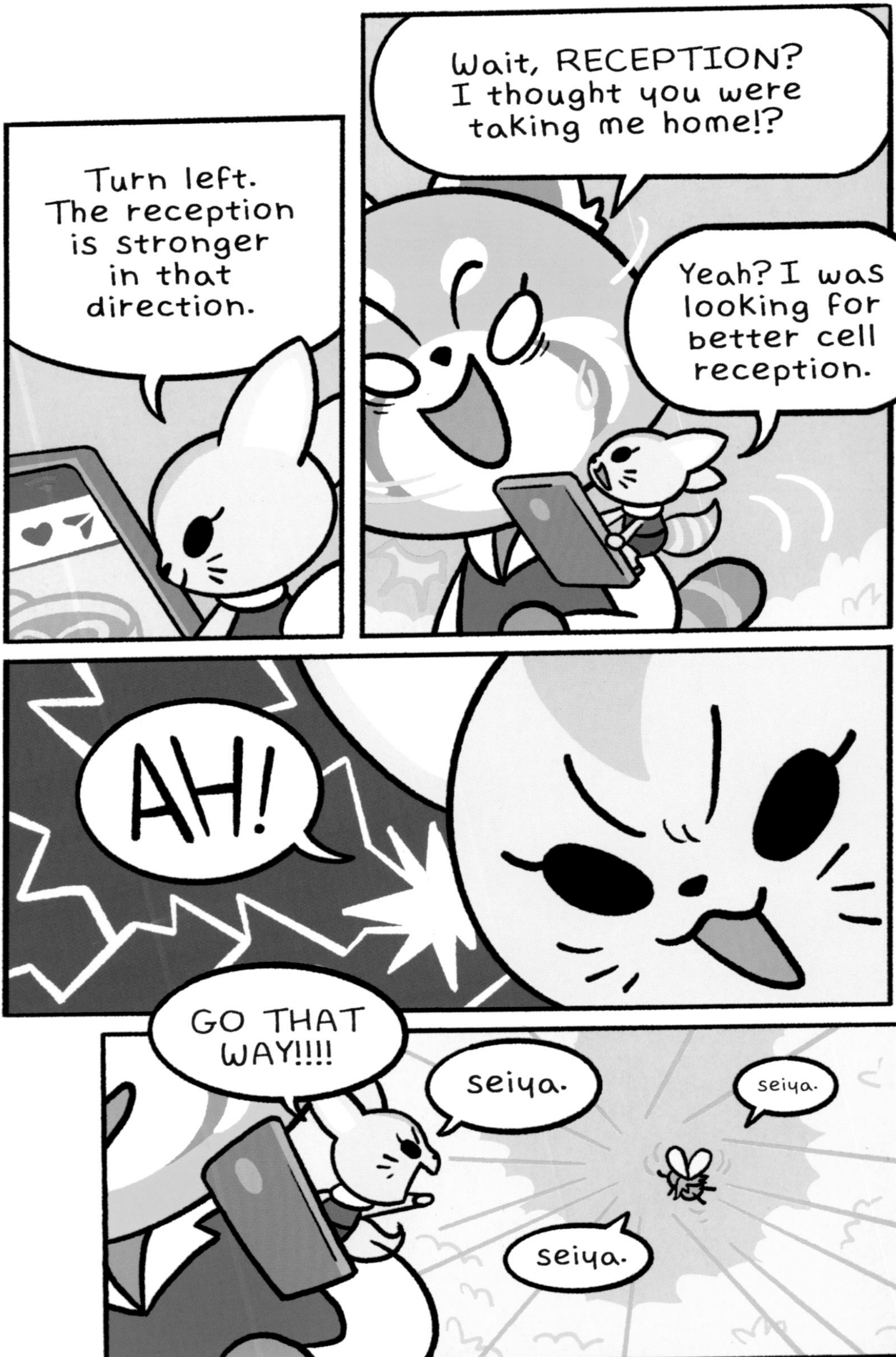
Turn left. The reception is stronger in that direction.
Wait, RECEPTION? I thought you were taking me home!?
Yeah? I was looking for better cell reception.
AH!
GO THAT WAY!!!!
seiya.
seiya.
seiya.

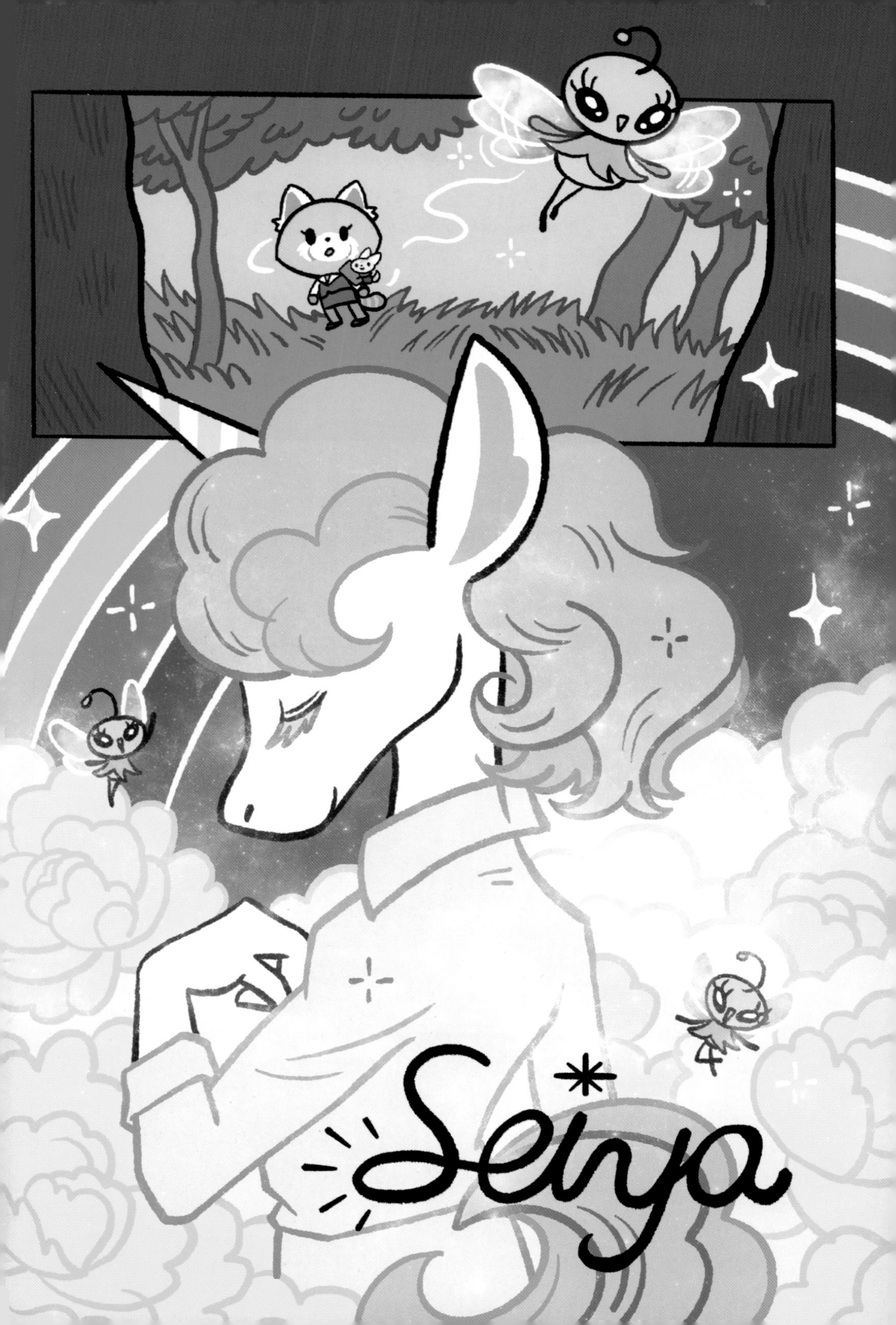
Senya

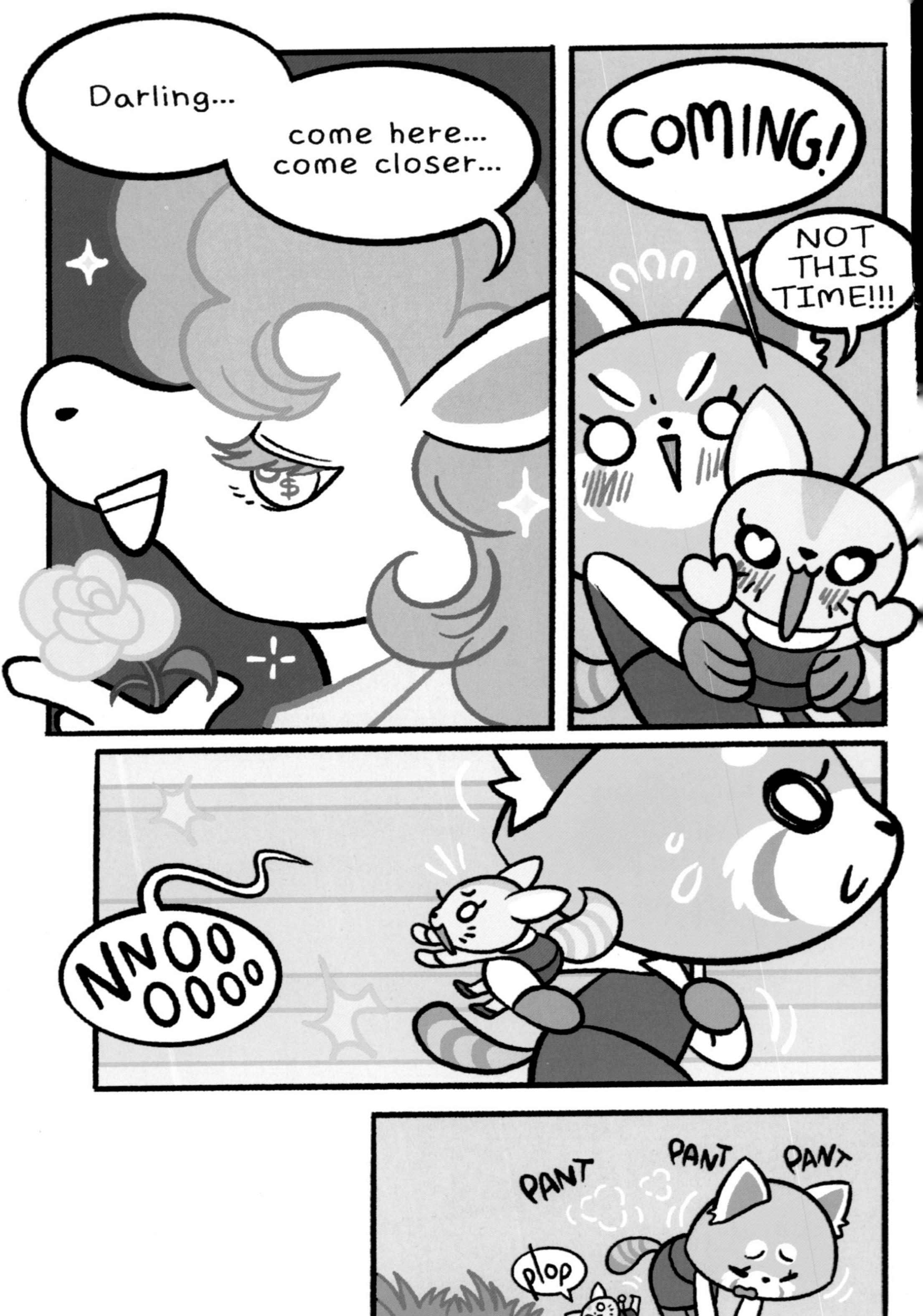
Darling...
come here... come closer...
COMING!
NOT THIS TIME!!!
NNOO OOOO
PANT
PANT
PANT
plop

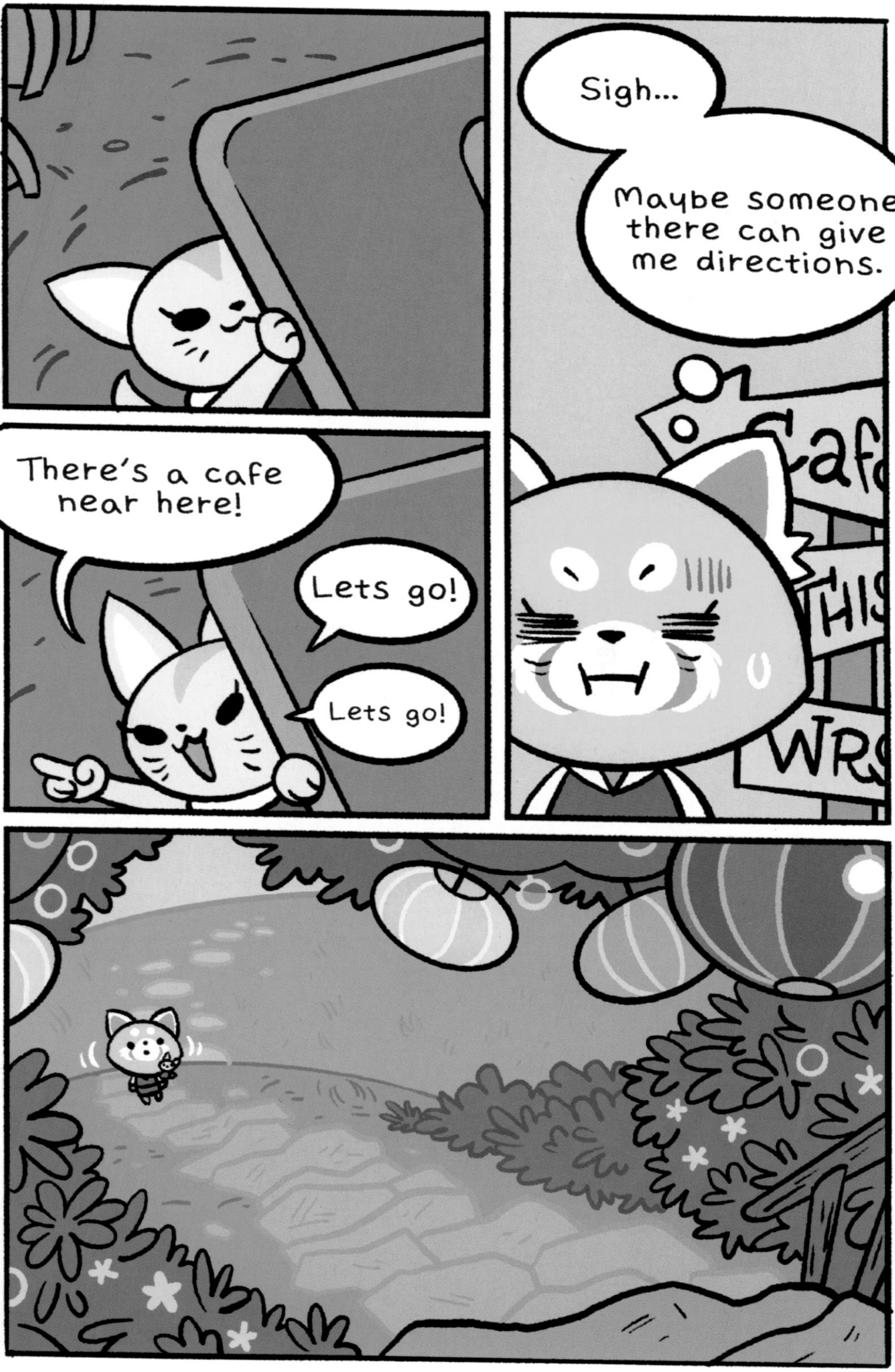
Sigh...
Maybe someone there can give me directions.
There's a cafe near here!
Lets go!
Lets go!
Cafe
THIS
WR

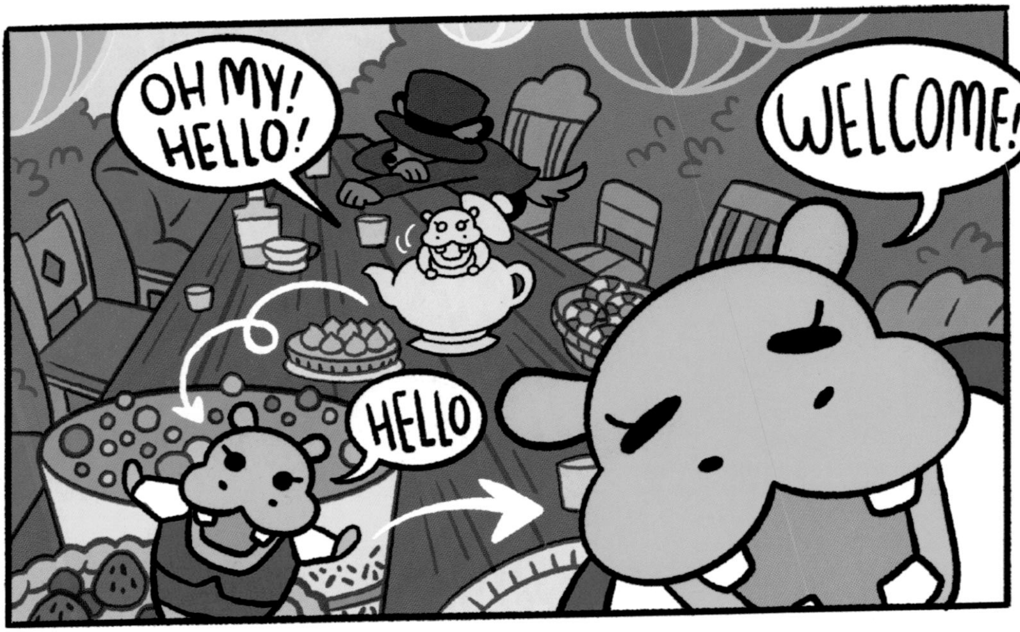
OH MY! HELLO!
WELCOME!
HELLO

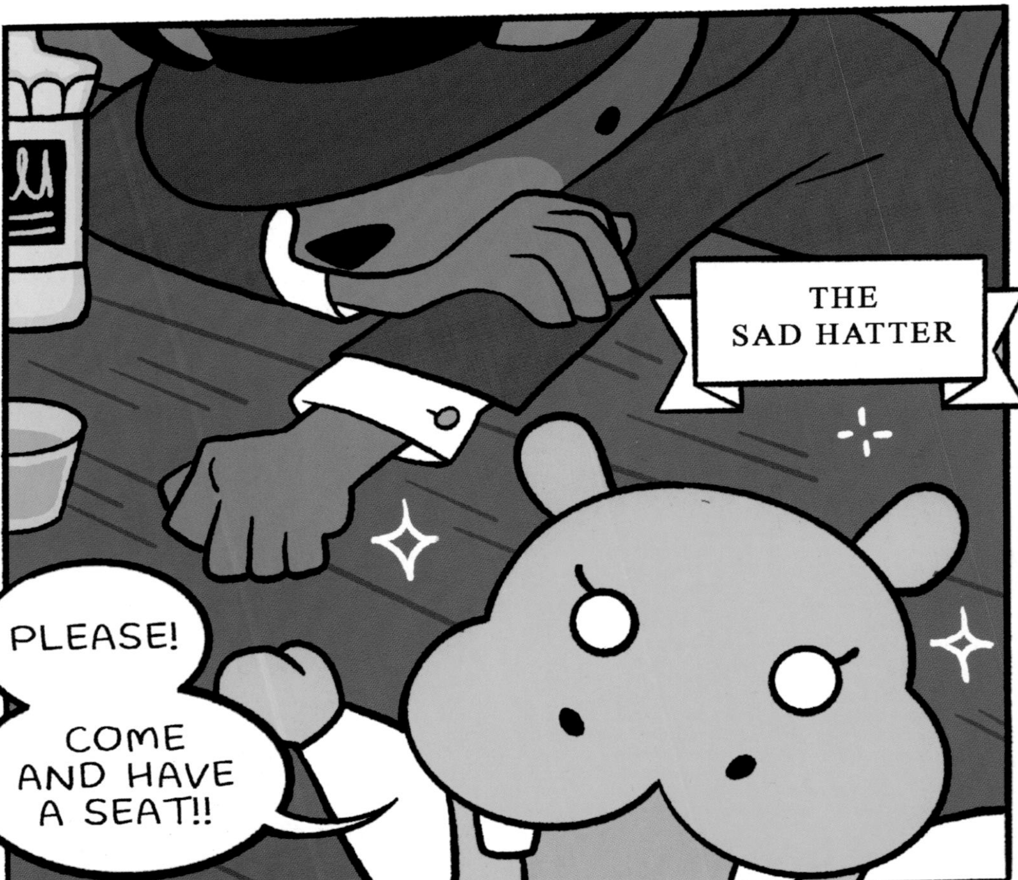
THE SAD HATTER
PLEASE!
COME AND HAVE A SEAT!!

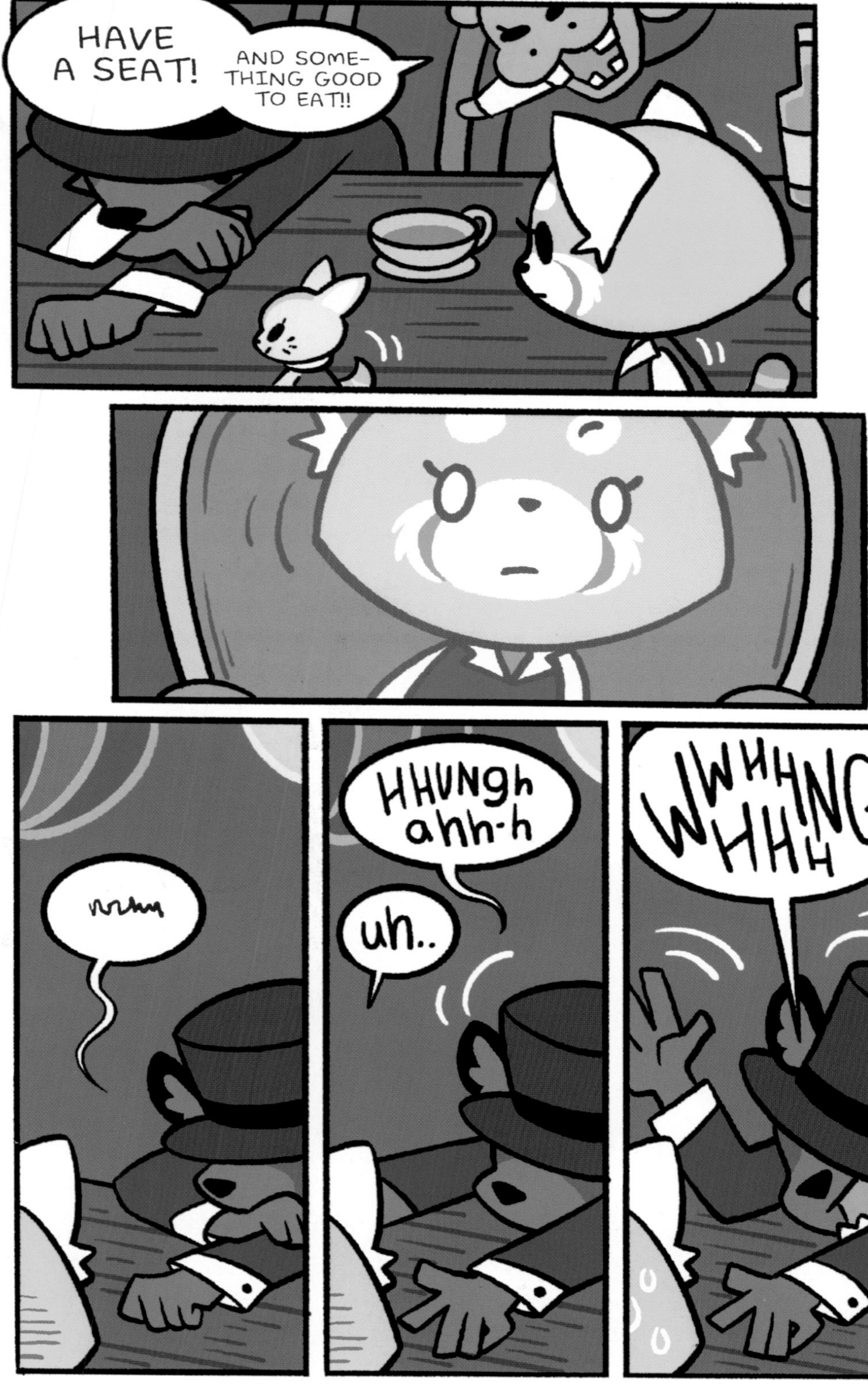
HAVE A SEAT!
AND SOME-THING GOOD TO EAT!!
HHUNGh ahh-h
uh..
WWHHNG WHHHH

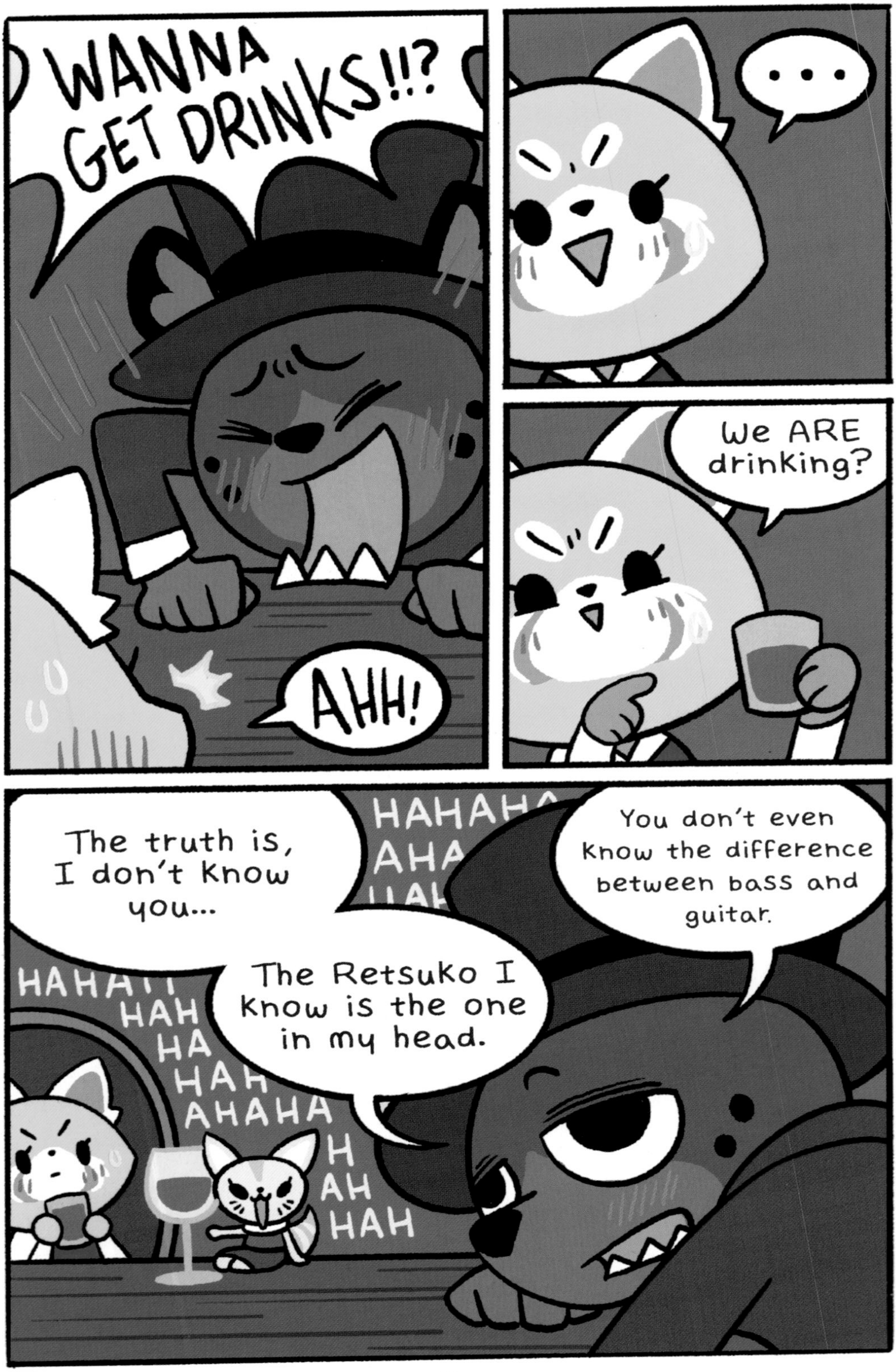

WANNA GET DRINKS!!?
AHH!
...
We ARE drinking?
The truth is, I don't know you...
The Retsuko I know is the one in my head.
You don't even know the difference between bass and guitar.
HAHAHA AHA HAHAH HAH HA HAH AHAHA H AH HAH

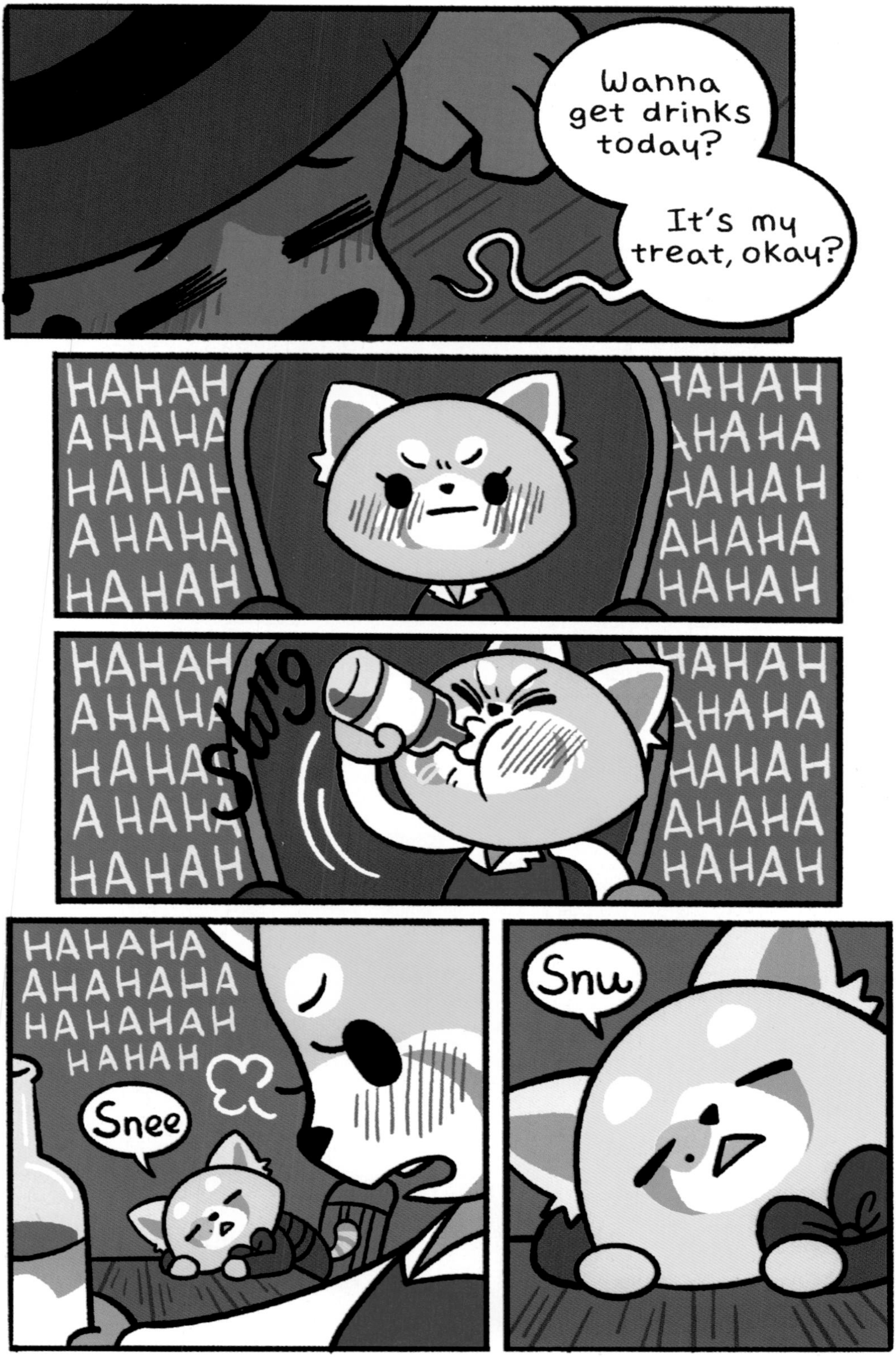
Wanna get drinks today?
It's my treat, okay?
HAHAH
AHAHA
HAHAH
AHAHA
HAHAH
HAHAH
AHAHA
HAHAH
AHAHA
HAHAH
Slug
HAHAHA
AHAHAHA
HAHAHAH
HAHAH
Snee
Snu

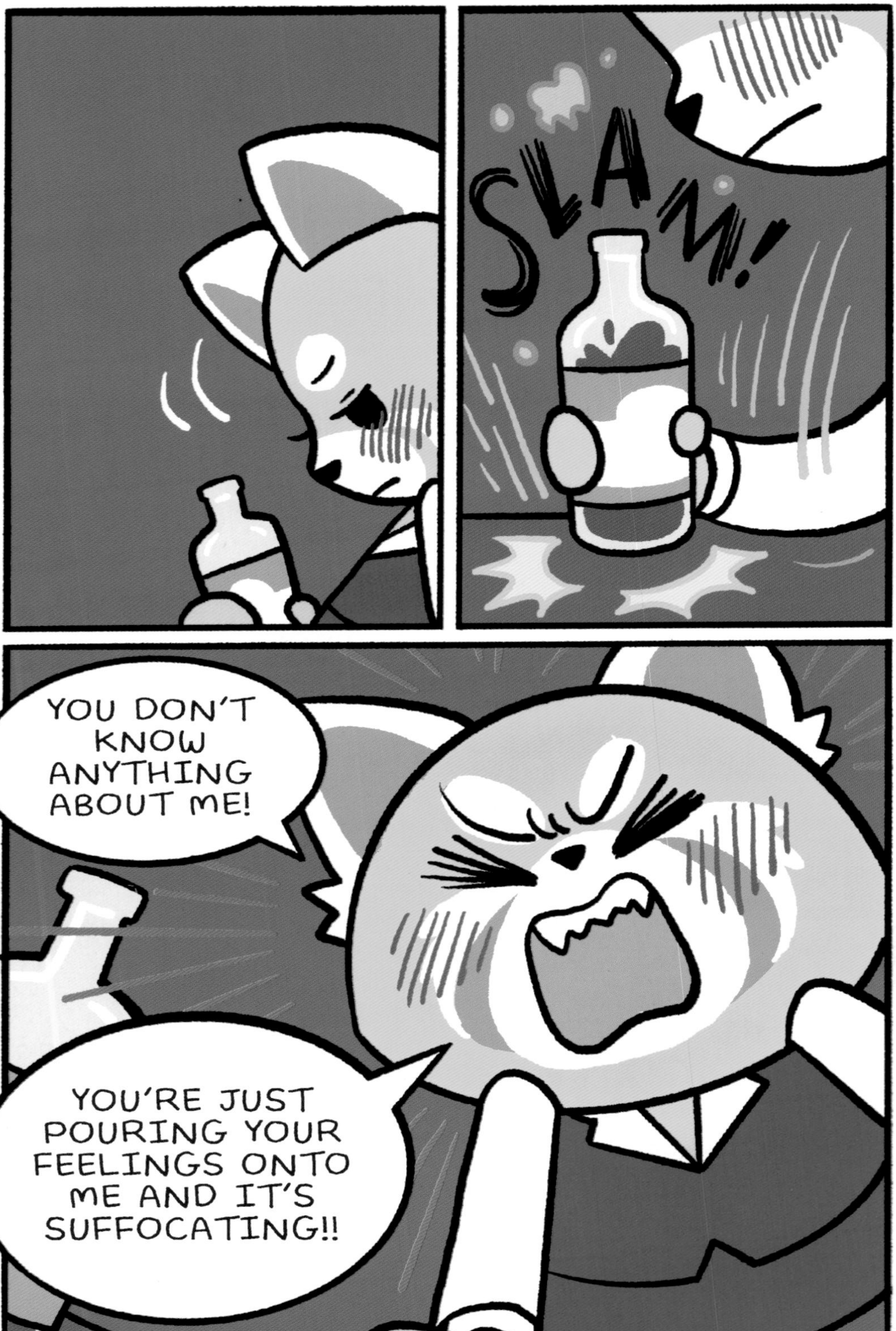
SLAM!
YOU DON'T KNOW ANYTHING ABOUT ME!
YOU'RE JUST POURING YOUR FEELINGS ONTO ME AND IT'S SUFFOCATING!!

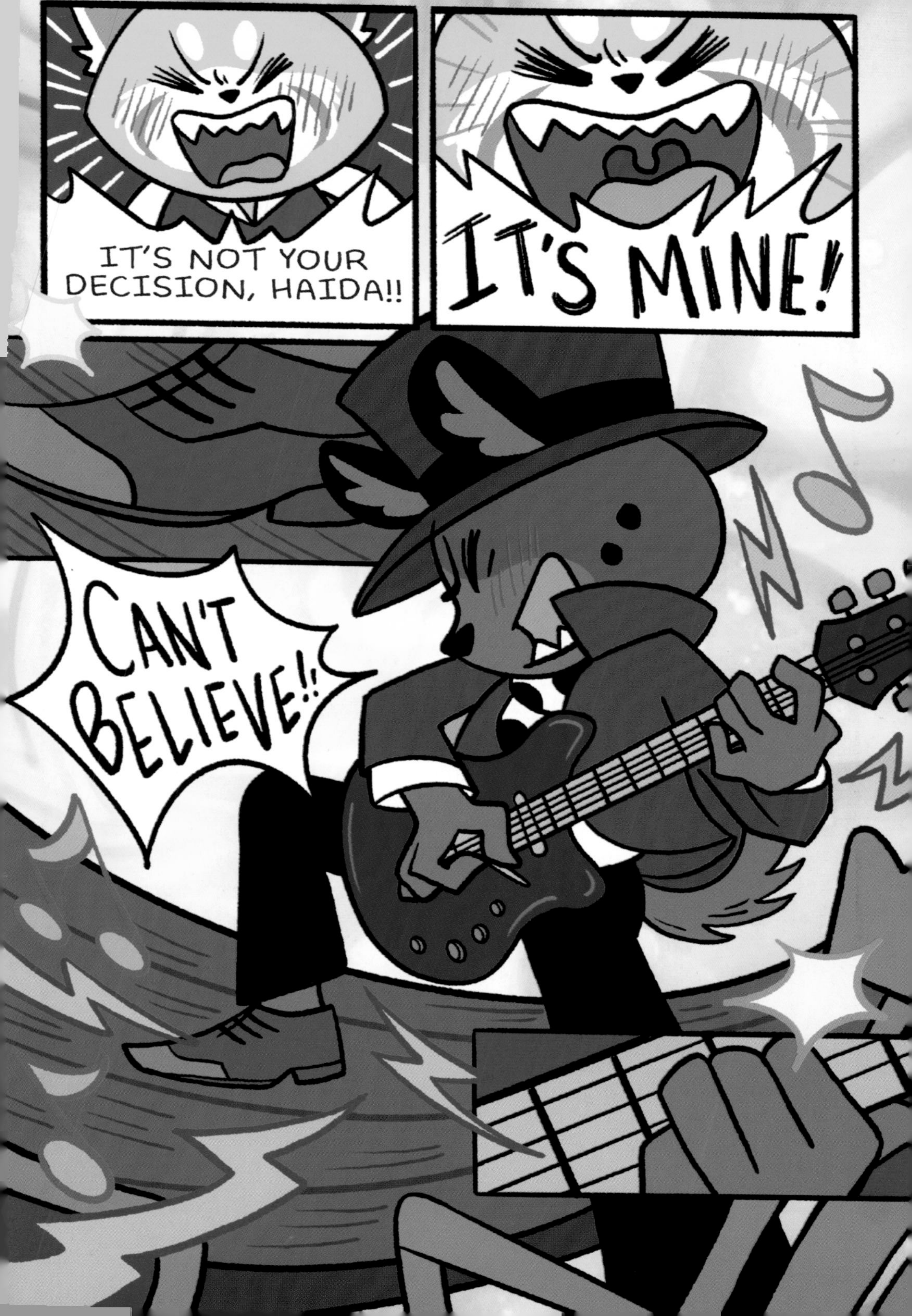
IT'S NOT YOUR DECISION, HAIDA!!
IT'S MINE!
CAN'T BELIEVE!!

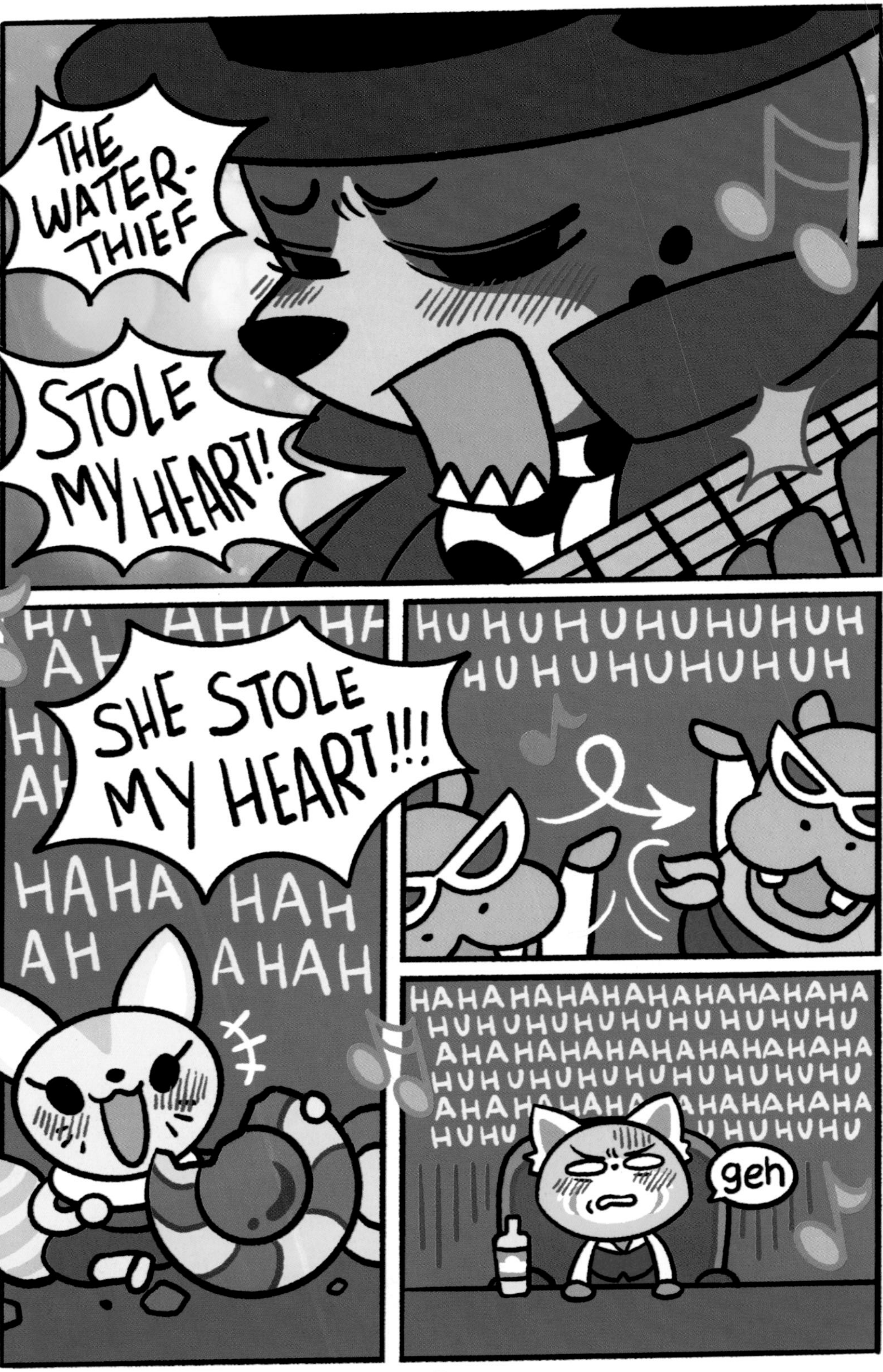
THE WATER-THIEF
STOLE MY HEART!
SHE STOLE MY HEART!!!
HUHUHUHUHUHUH
HAHAHAHAHAHAHAHAHA
HUHUHUHUHUHUHUHUHU
geh

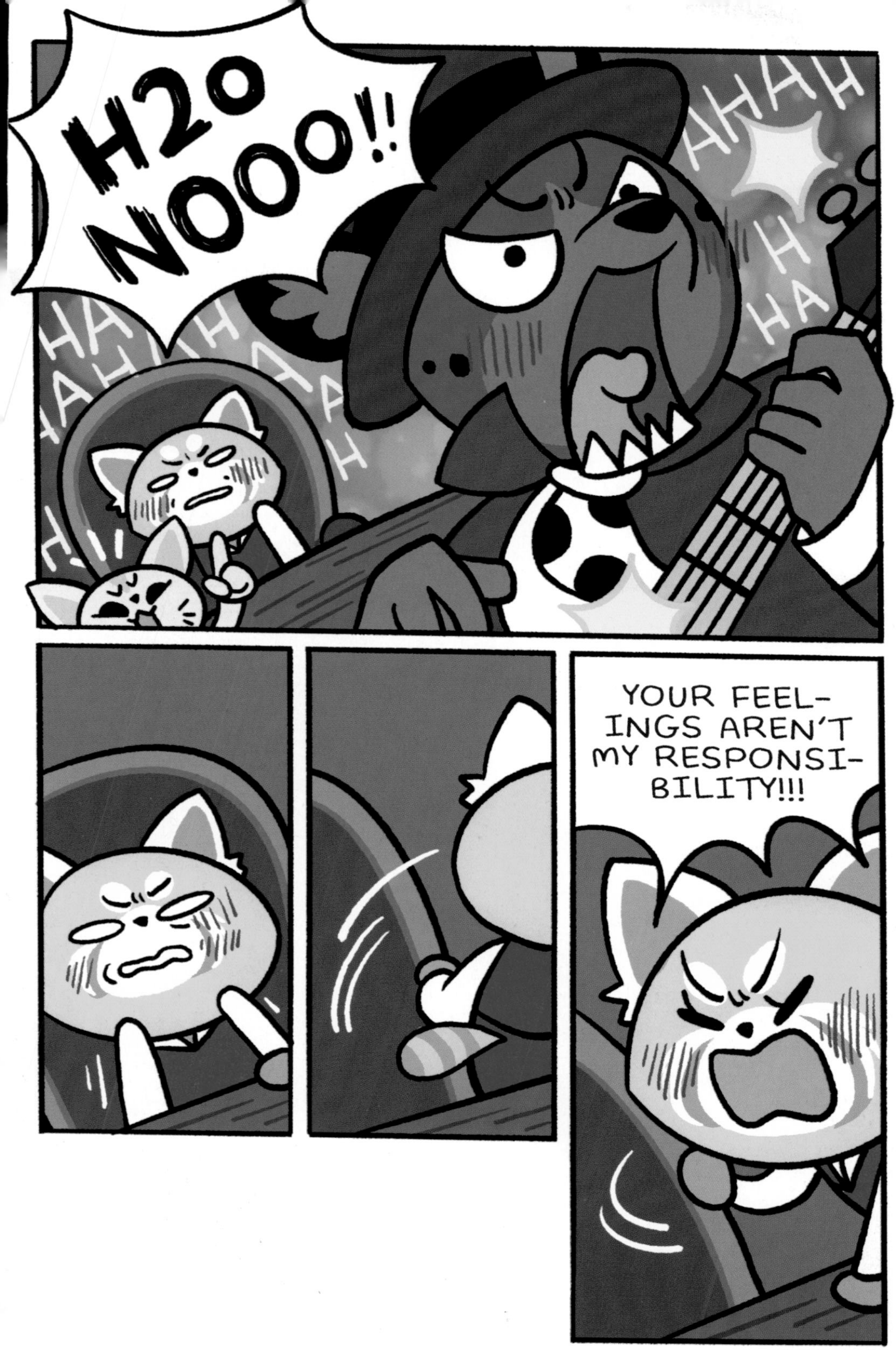
H2O NOOO!!
HAHAHAHAHAH
HAHAHAHAH
HAHAH
HAH!!
YOUR FEEL-
INGS AREN'T
MY RESPONSI-
BILITY!!!

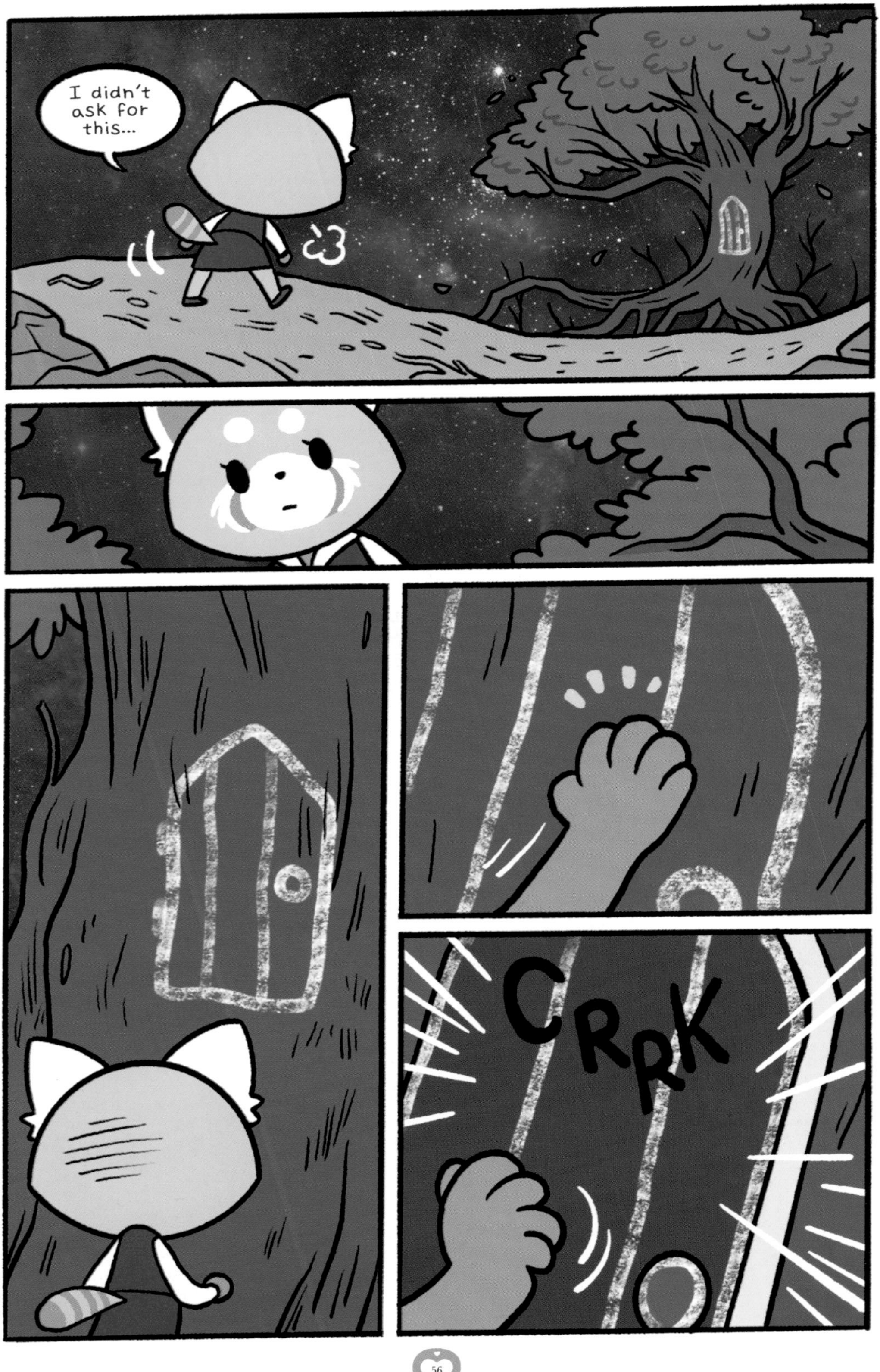
I didn't ask for this...
CRRK

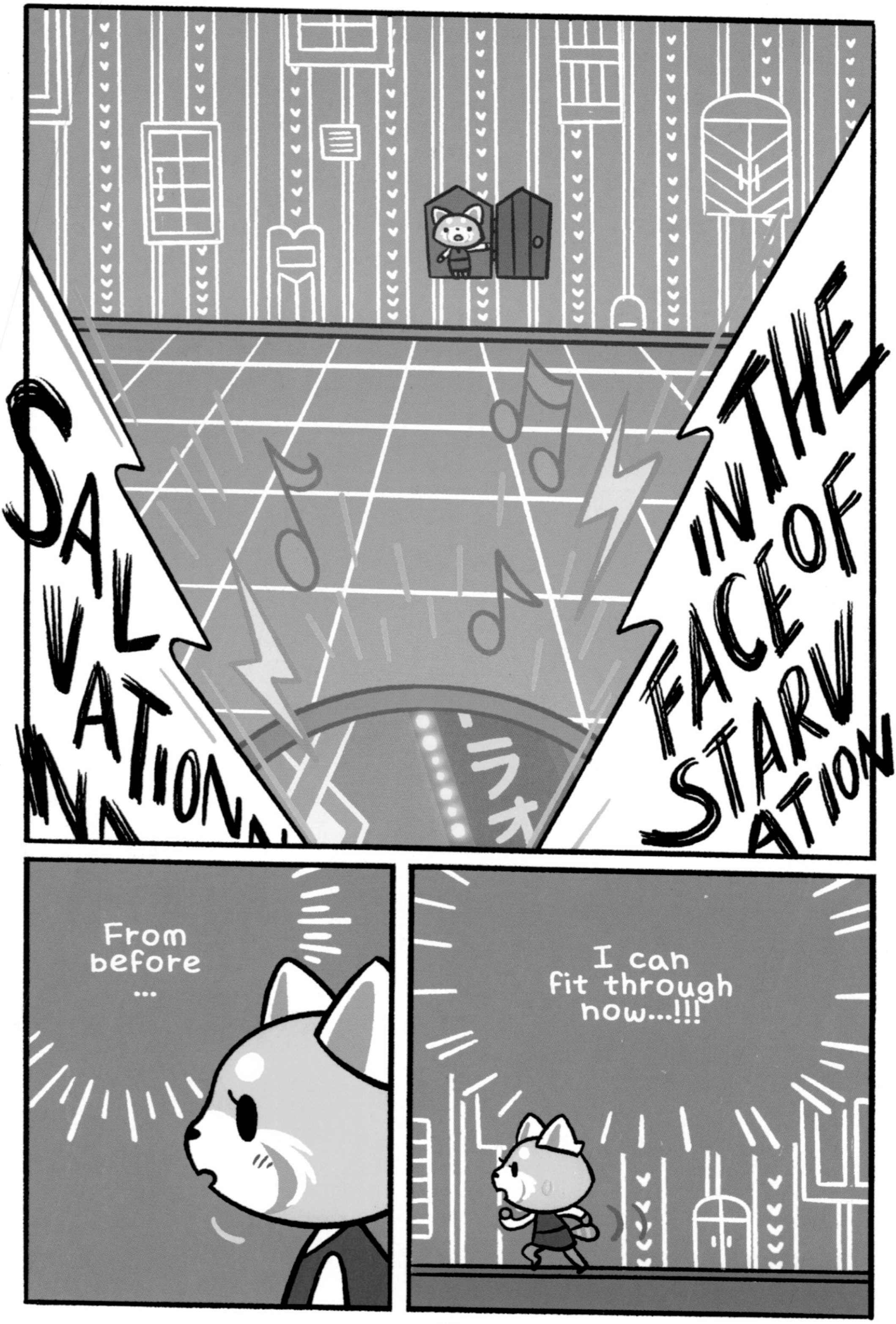
SALVATIONNN
IN THE FACE OF STARVATION
ラオ
From before ...
I can fit through now...!!!

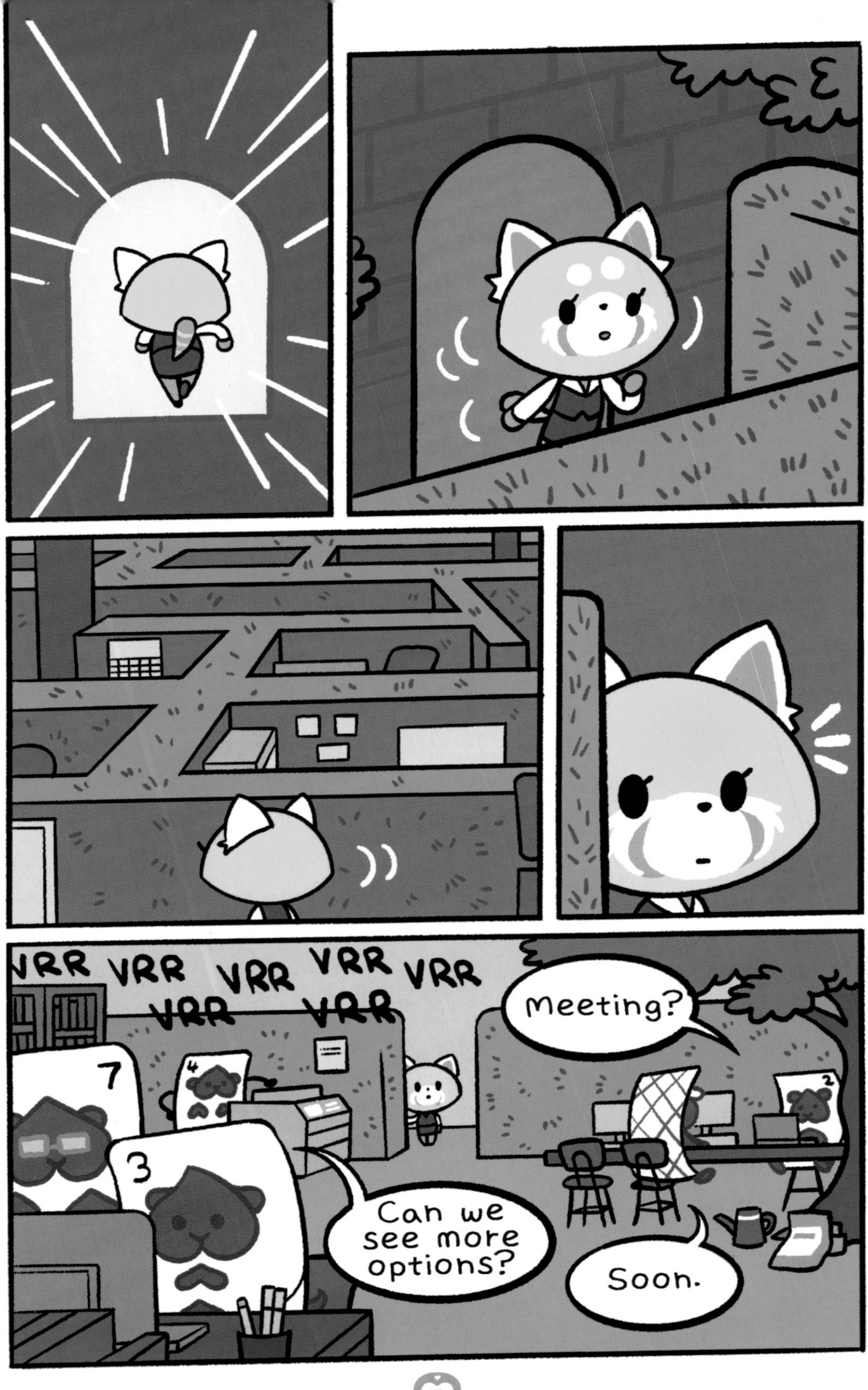
VRR VRR VRR VRR VRR
VRR VRR
Meeting?
Can we see more options?
Soon.

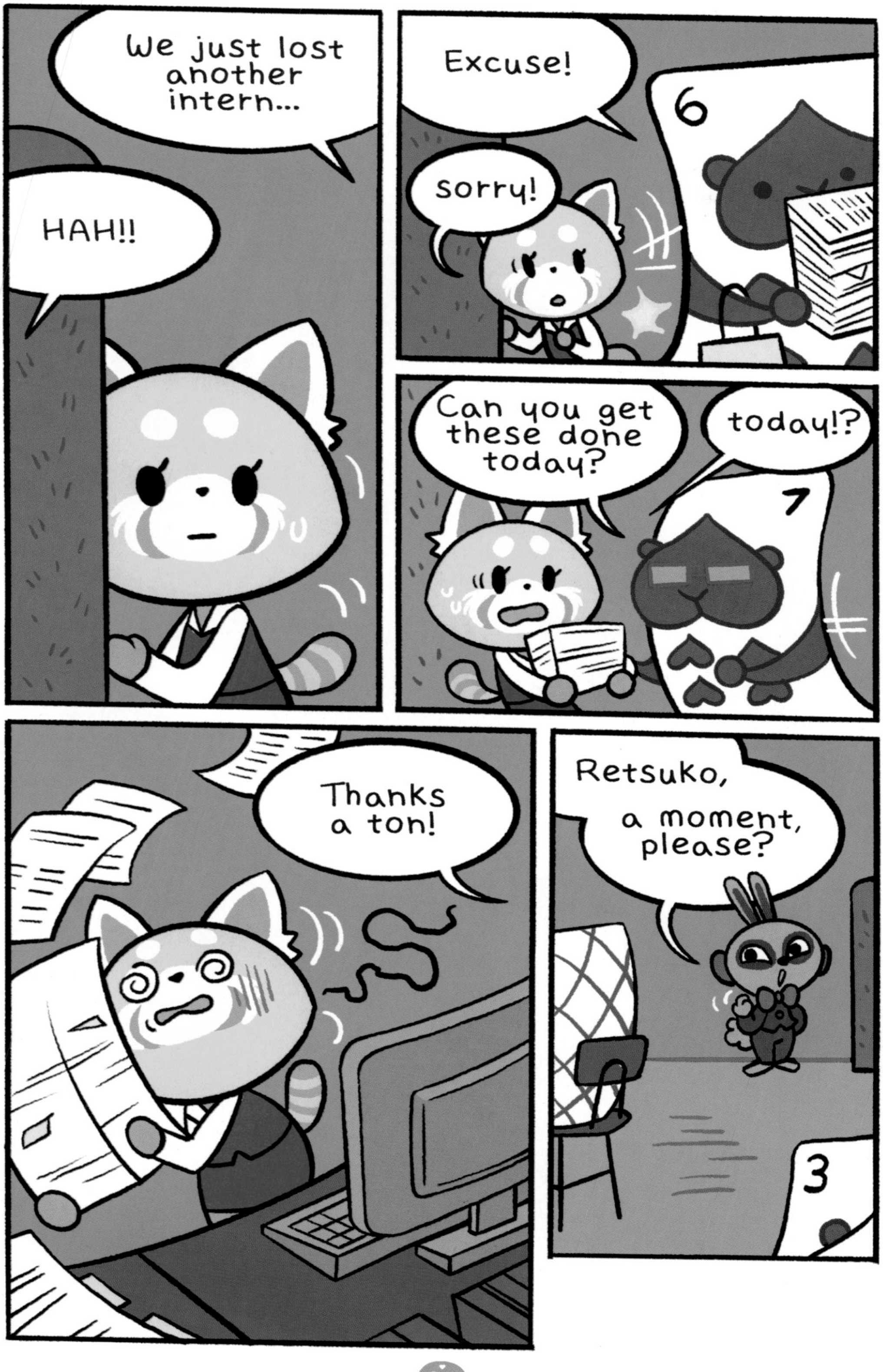
We just lost another intern...
HAH!!
Excuse!
sorry!
6
Can you get these done today?
today!?
7
Thanks a ton!
Retsuko, a moment, please?
3

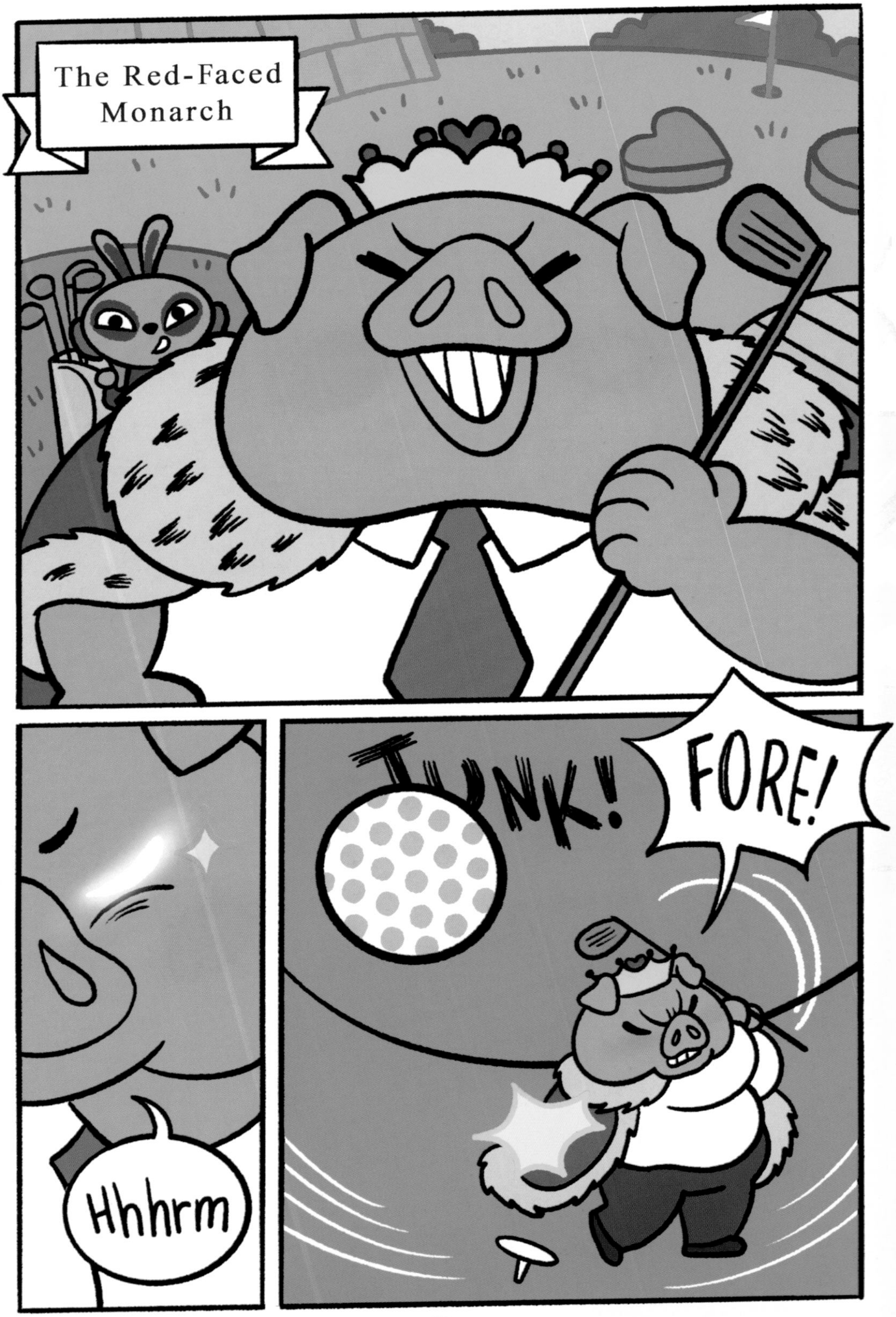
The Red-Faced Monarch
Hhhrm
FORE!

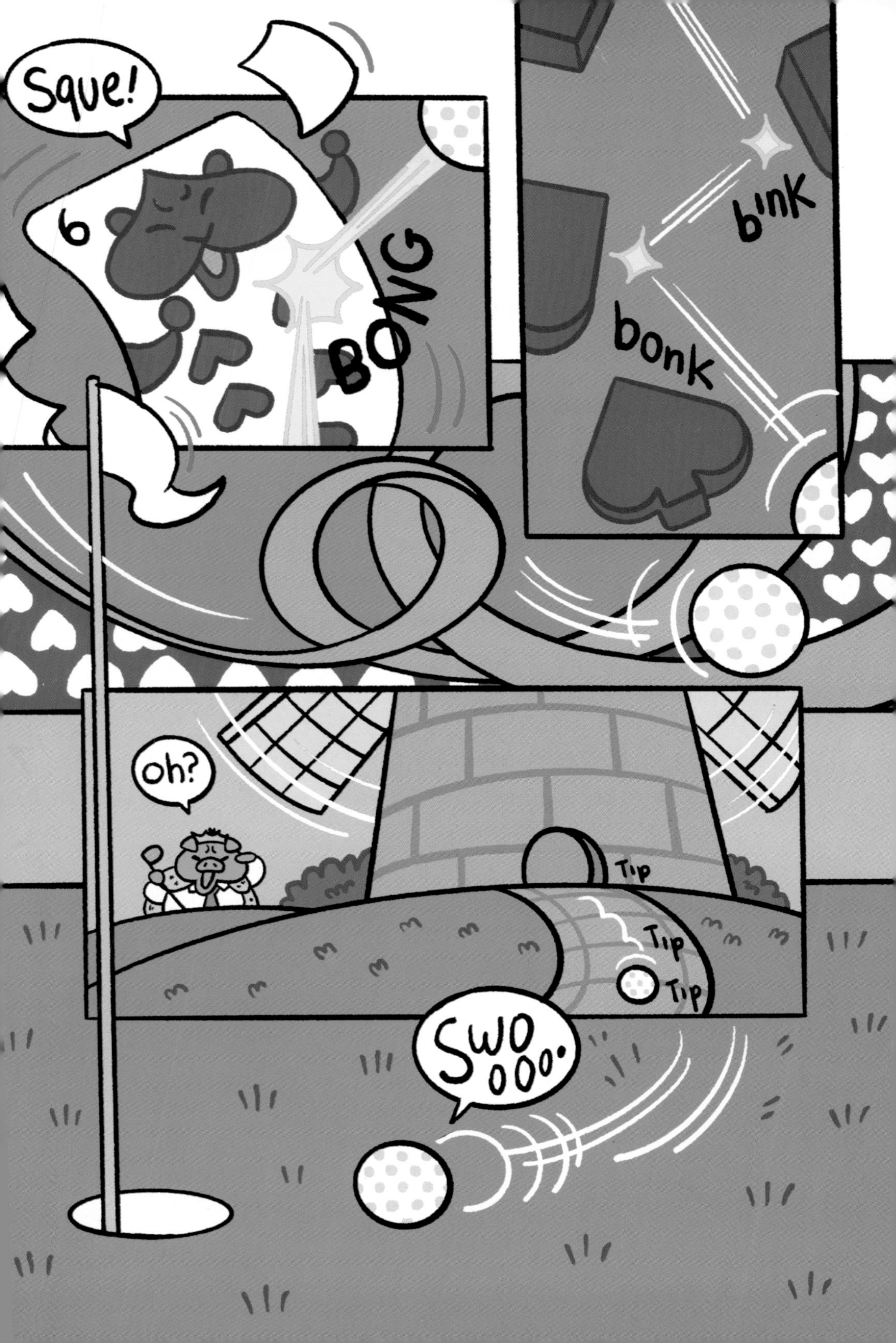
Sque!
6
BONG
bink
bonk
oh?
Tip
Tip
Tip
SWOooo.

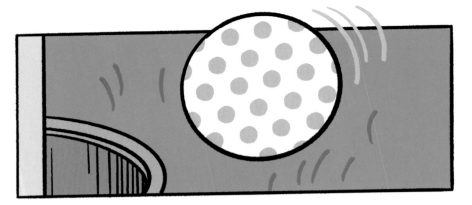

OH?

MISS!

grrrr...

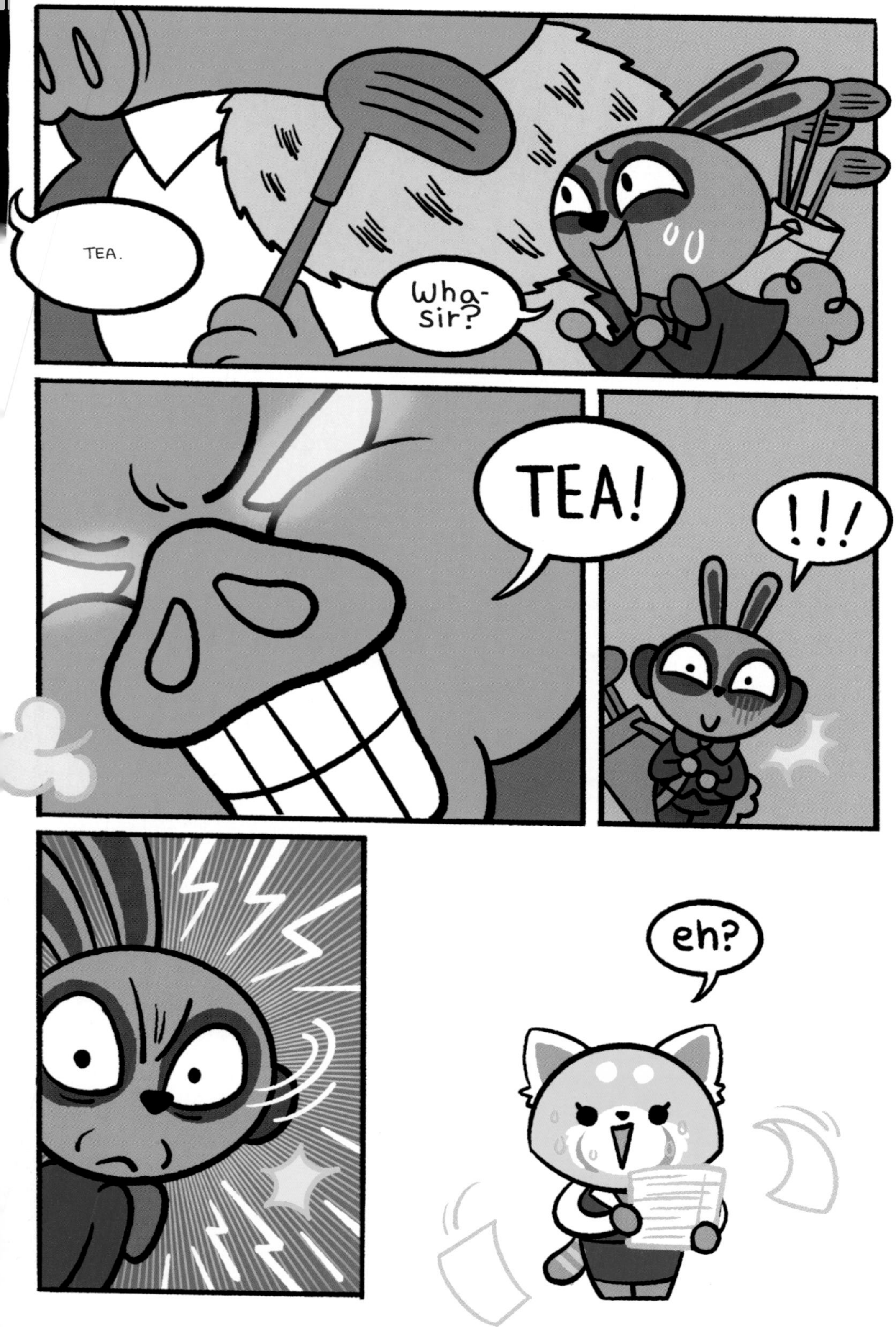

TEA.
Wha-sir?
TEA!
!!!
eh?

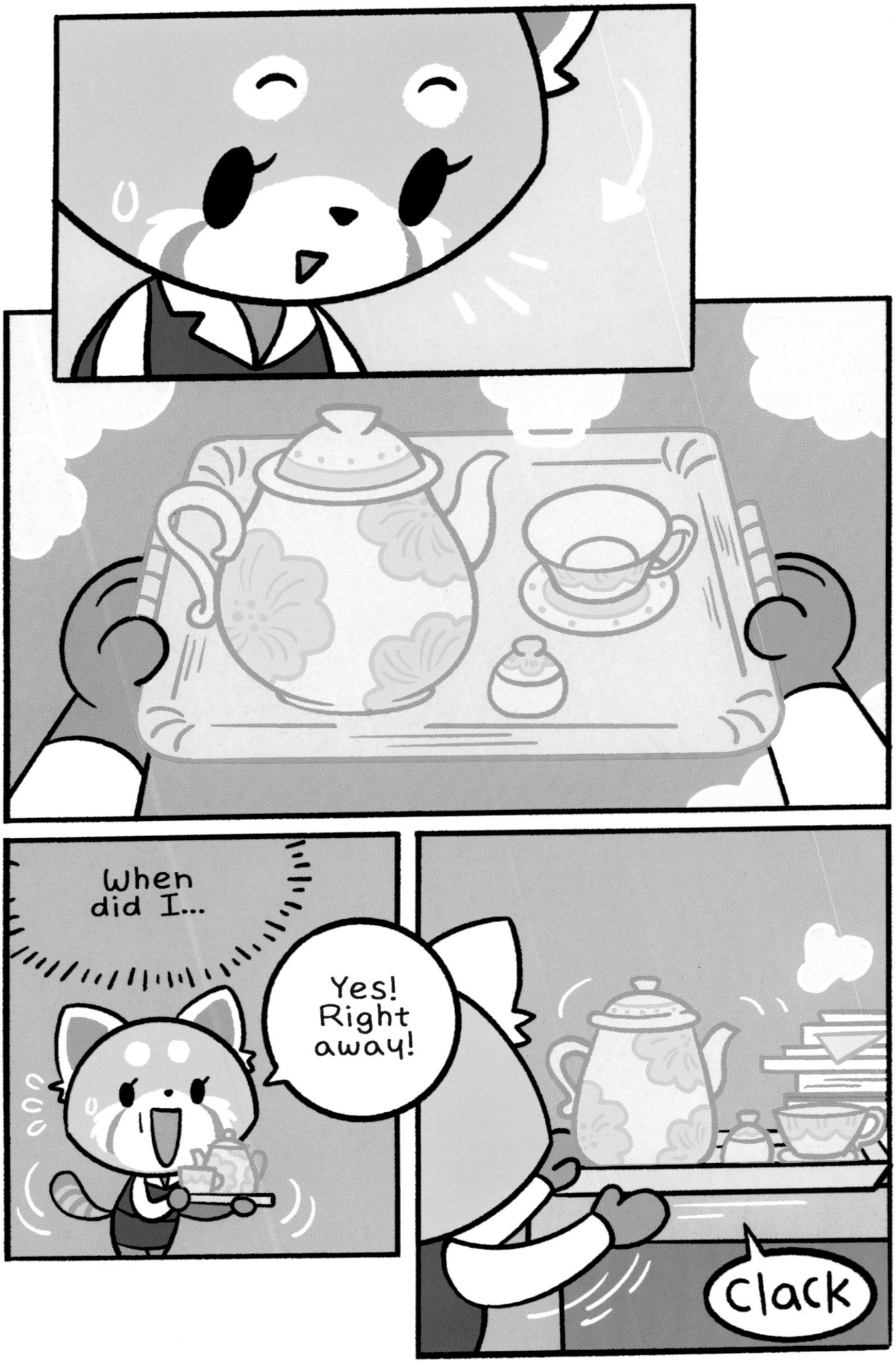
When did I...
Yes! Right away!
Clack

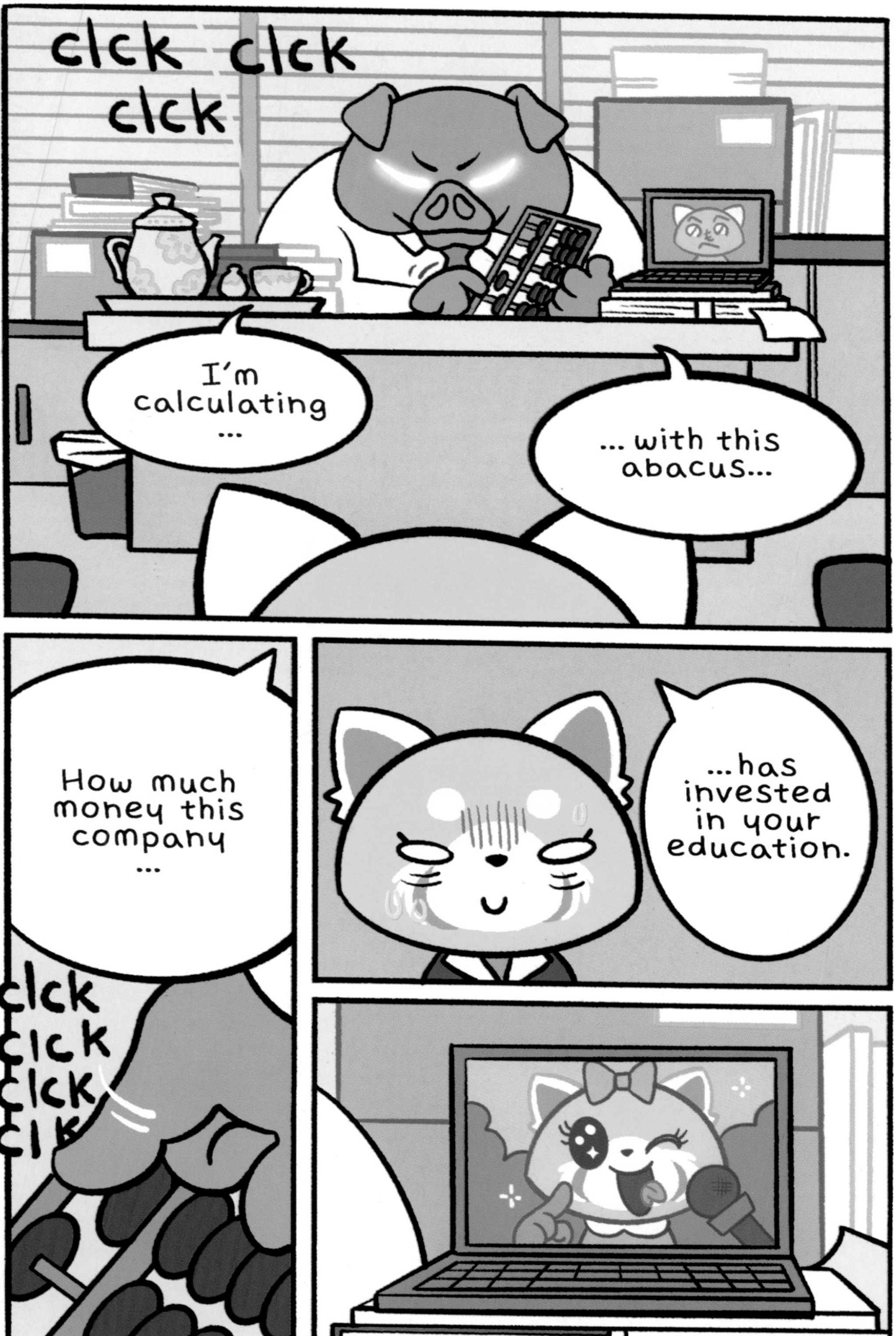
clck clck
clck
I'm calculating ...
... with this abacus...
How much money this company ...
... has invested in your education.
clck
clck
clck
clk

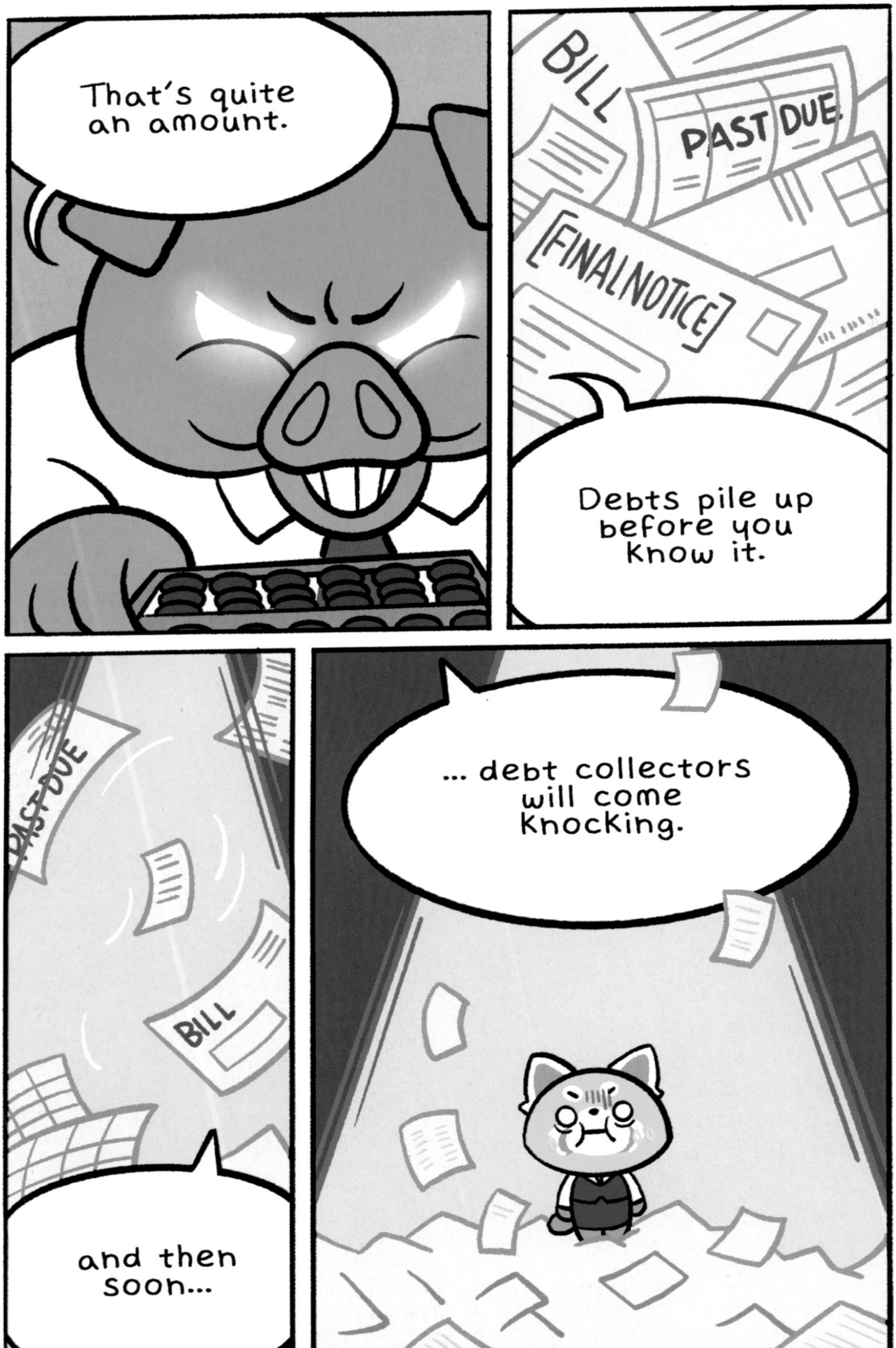
That's quite an amount.
BILL
PAST DUE
FINALNOTICE
Debts pile up before you know it.
PAST DUE
BILL
and then soon...
... debt collectors will come knocking.

Debts to your parents.

Debts to yourself.

Debts to society.

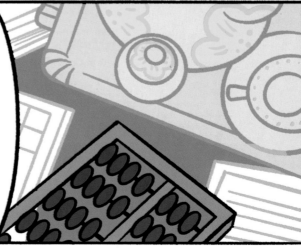

An average person's life is long and boring, but once someone messes up, they keep doing it, and the more mistakes there are, the more people suffer.

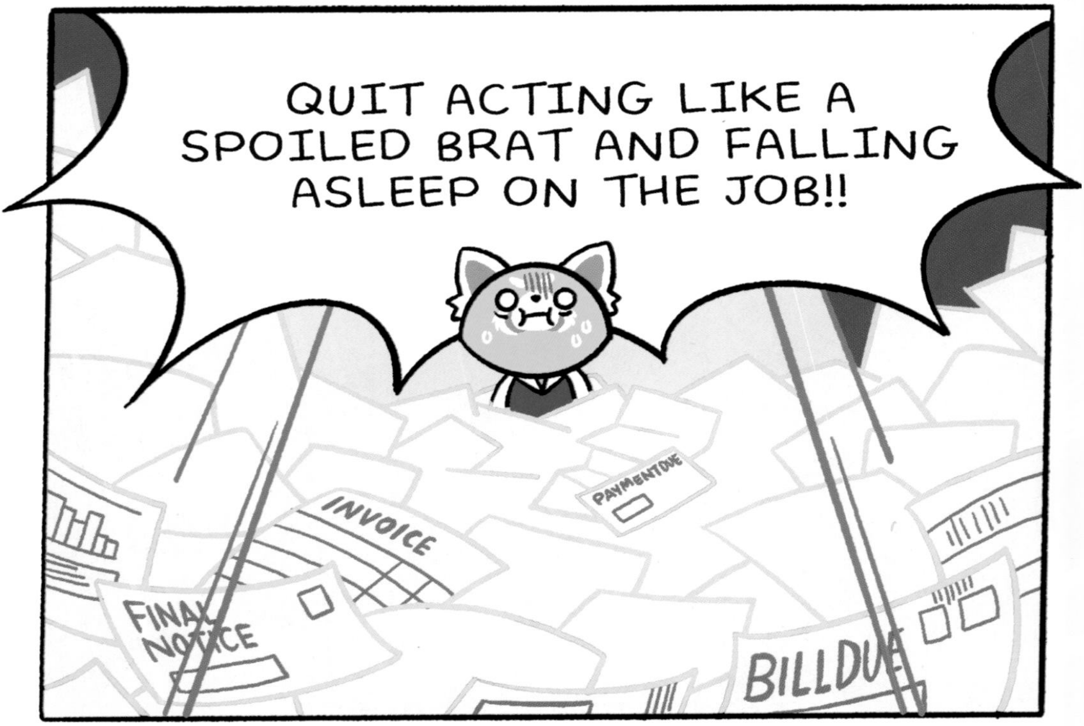
QUIT ACTING LIKE A SPOILED BRAT AND FALLING ASLEEP ON THE JOB!!
PAYMENT DUE
INVOICE
FINAL NOTICE
BILLDUE

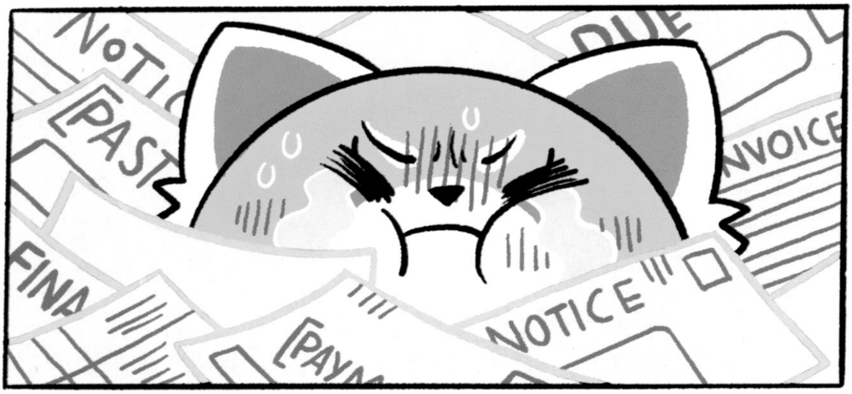
NOTICE

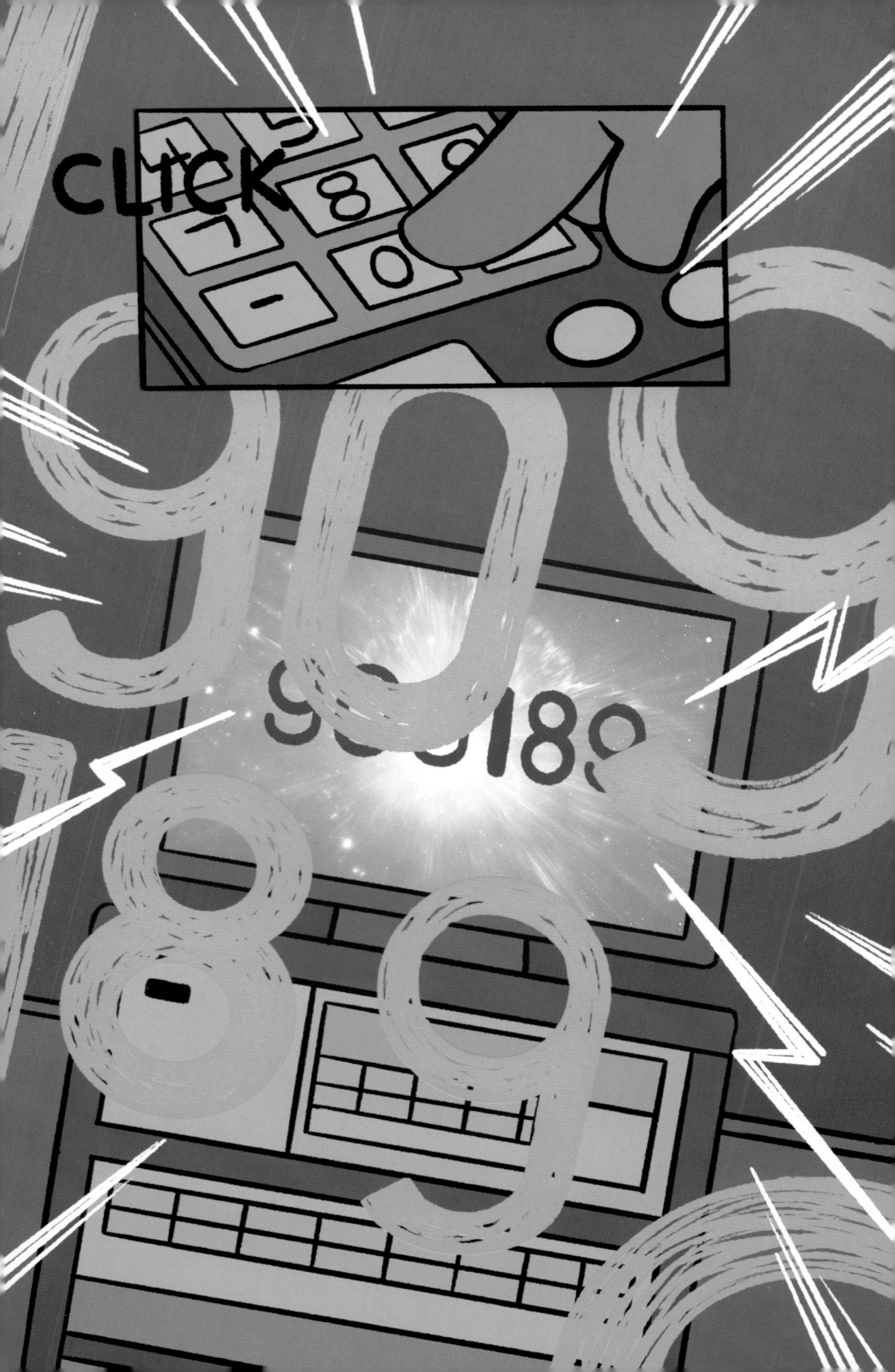
CLICK

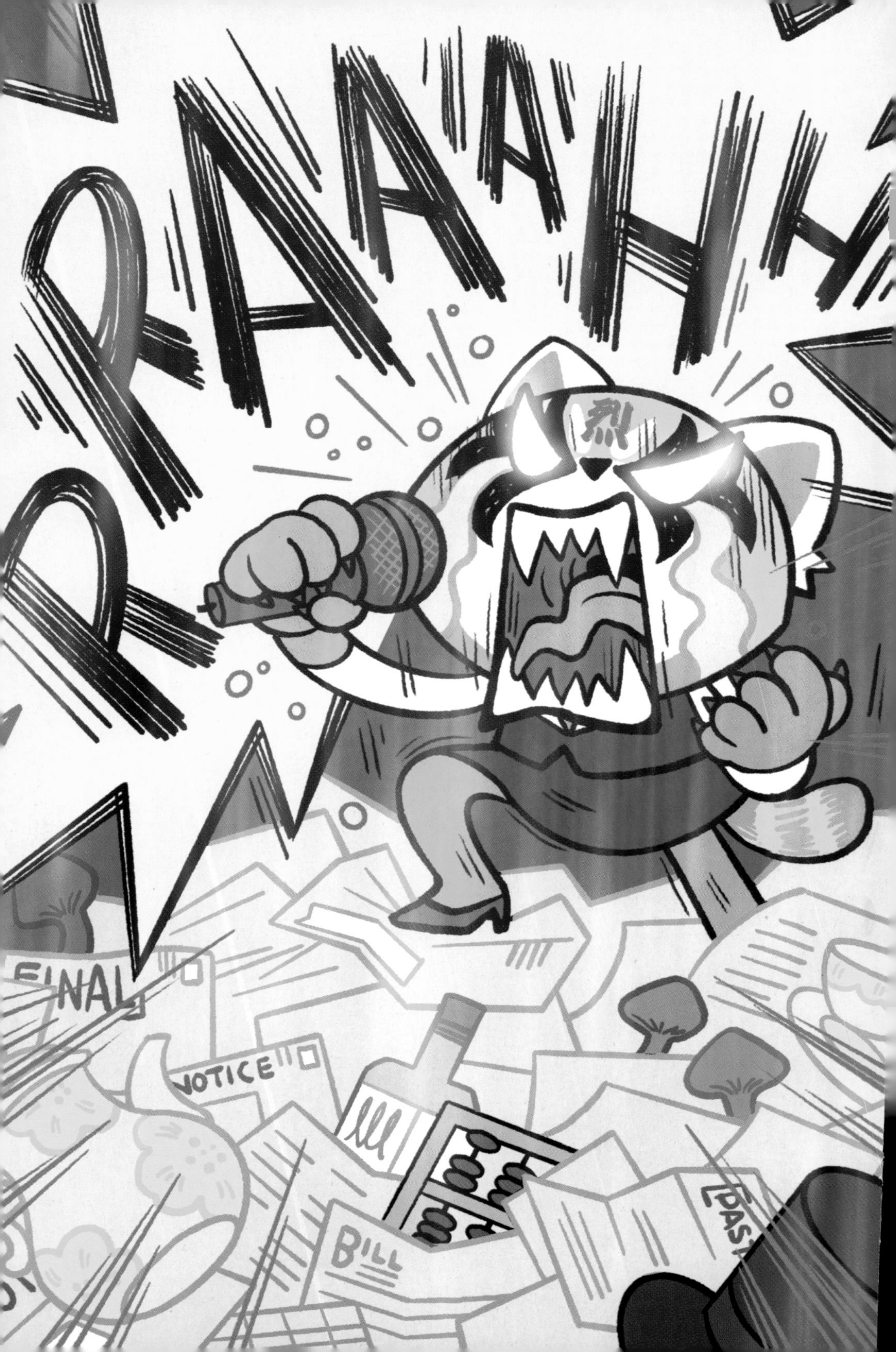
RAAAHH
烈
FINAL
NOTICE
BILL

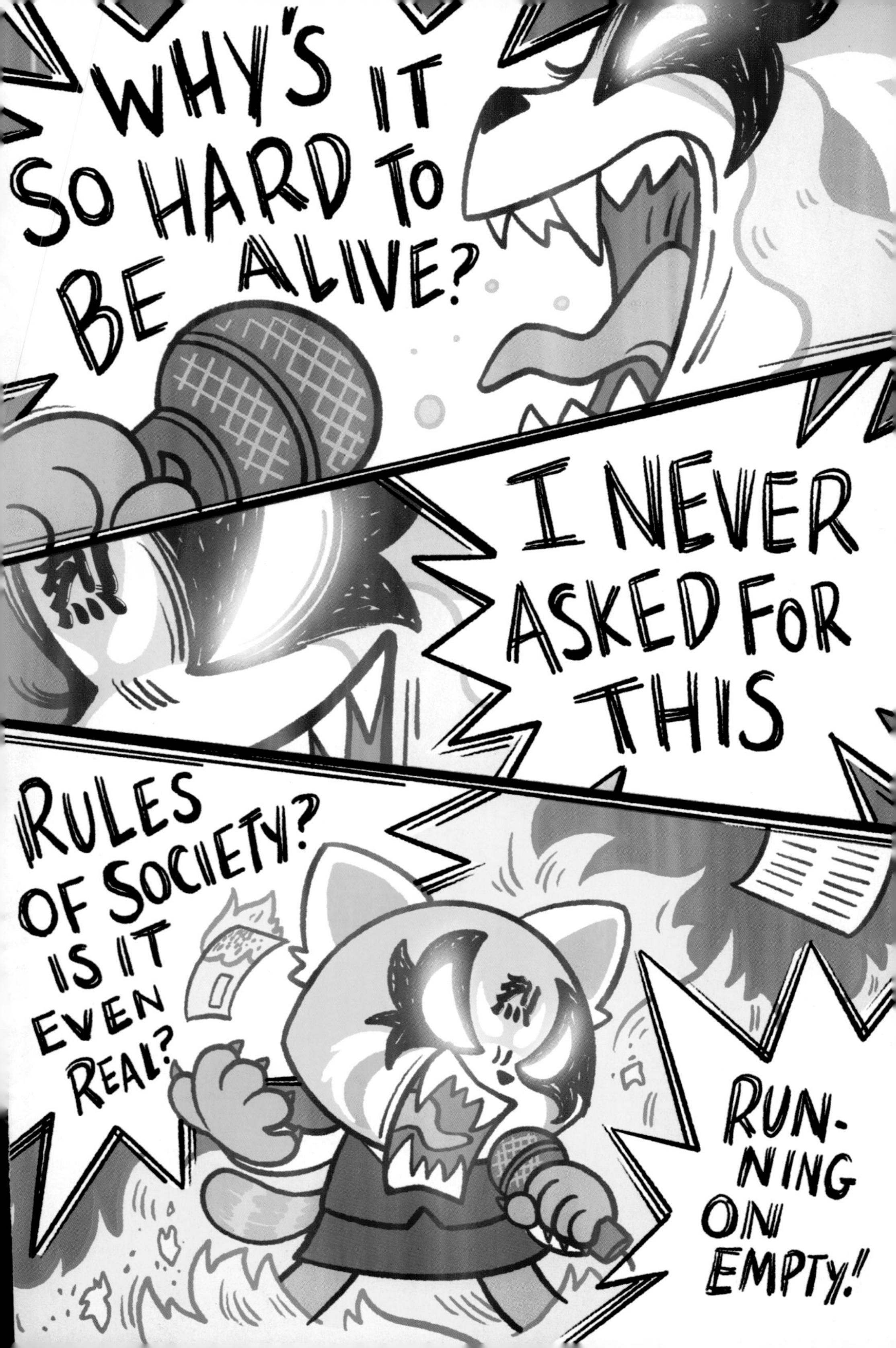
WHY'S IT SO HARD TO BE ALIVE?
I NEVER ASKED FOR THIS
RULES OF SOCIETY? IS IT EVEN REAL?
RUN-NING ON EMPTY!

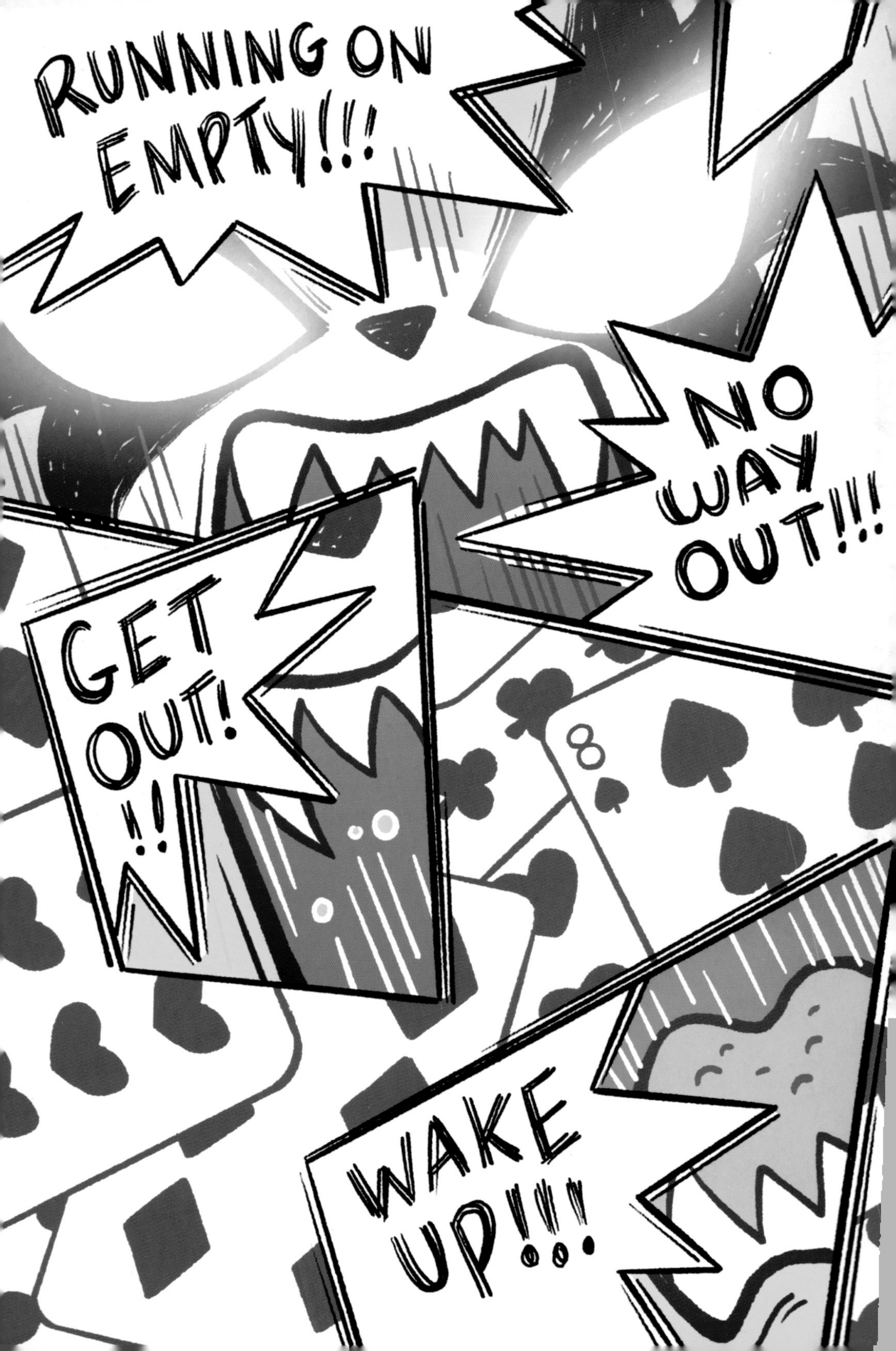
RUNNING ON EMPTY!!!
NO WAY OUT!!!!
GET OUT!!!
WAKE UP!!!!

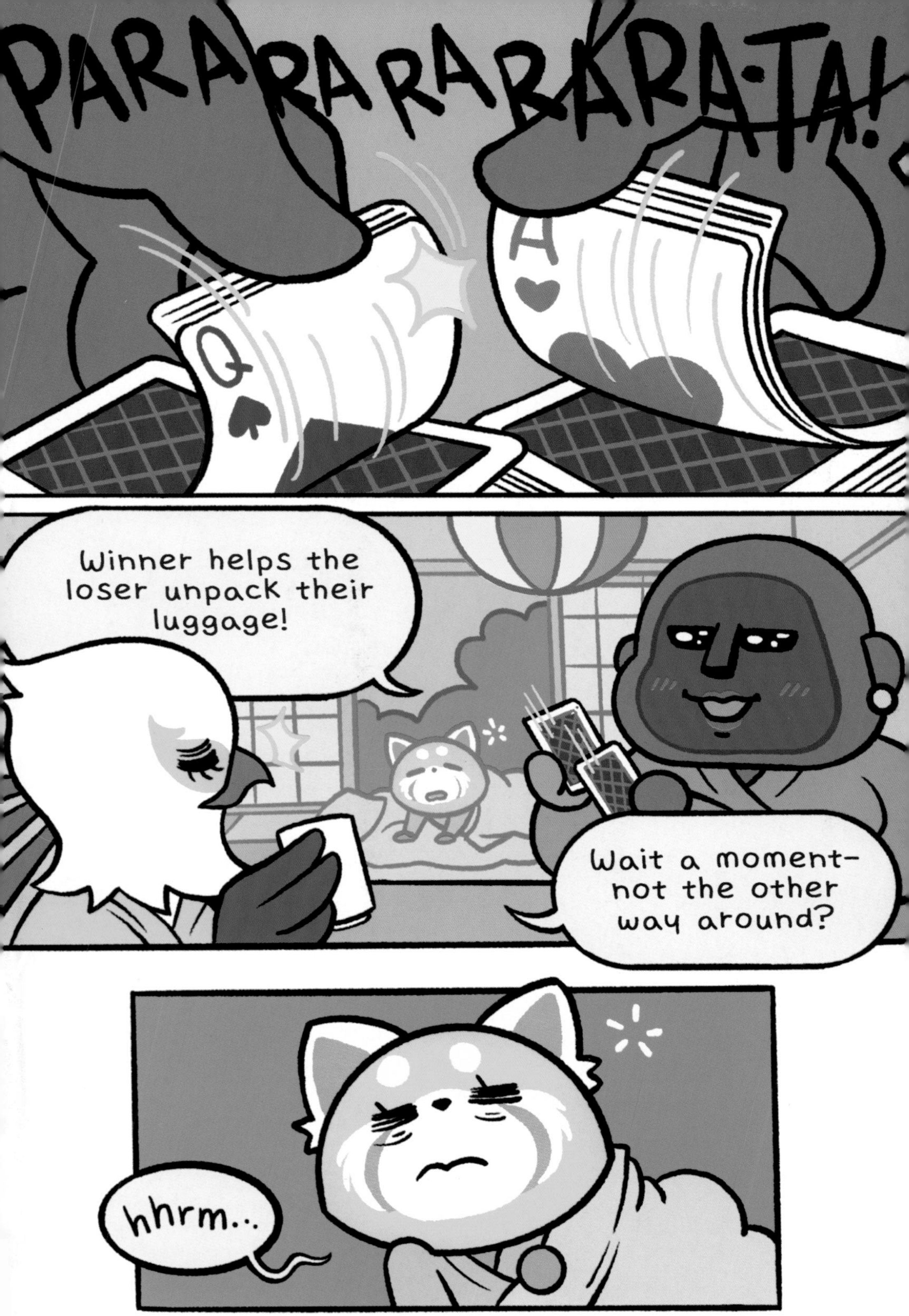
PARARARARARARA-TA!
Winner helps the loser unpack their luggage!
Wait a moment- not the other way around?
hhrm...

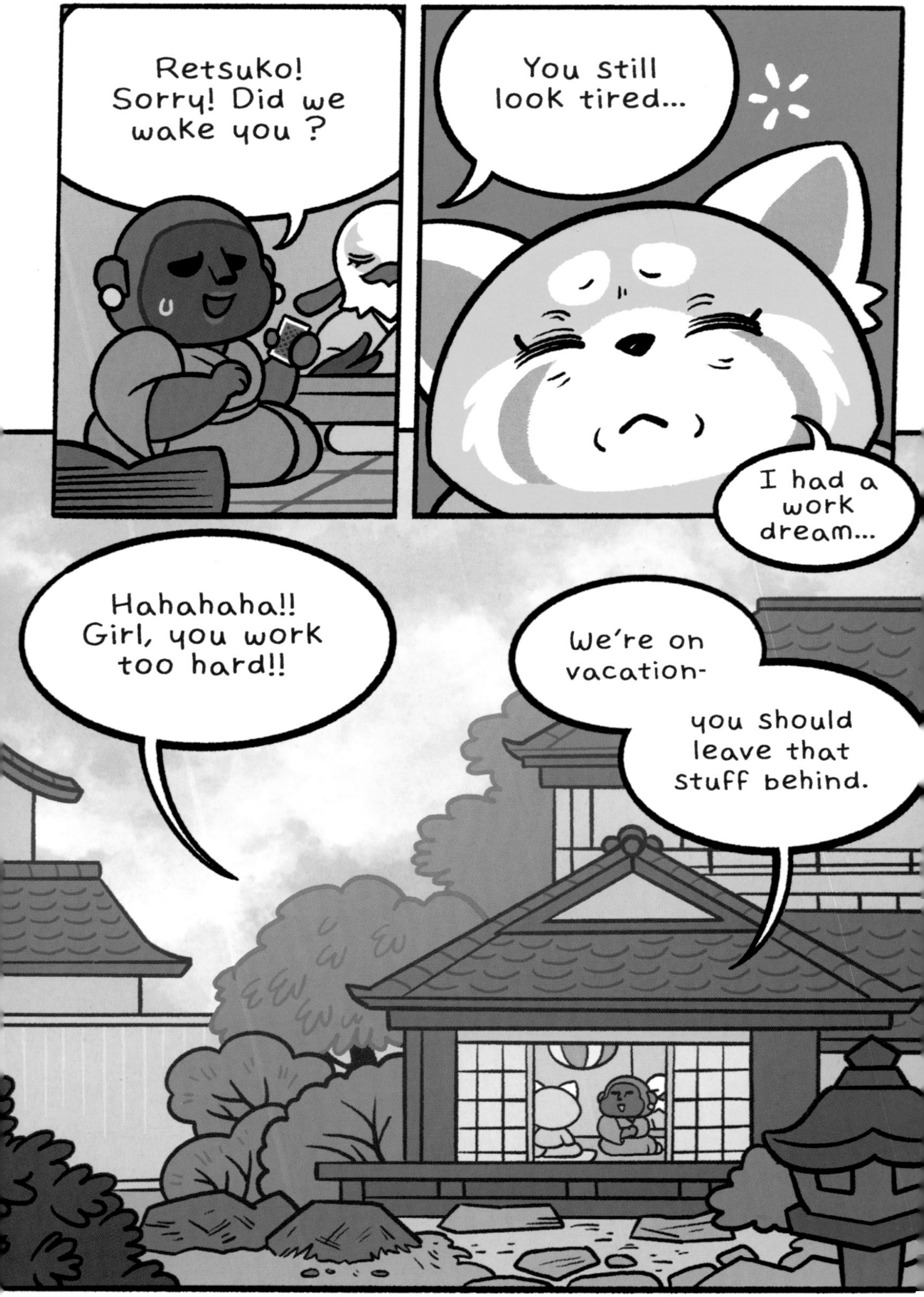
Retsuko! Sorry! Did we wake you ?
You still look tired...
I had a work dream...
Hahahaha!! Girl, you work too hard!!
We're on vacation-
you should leave that stuff behind.

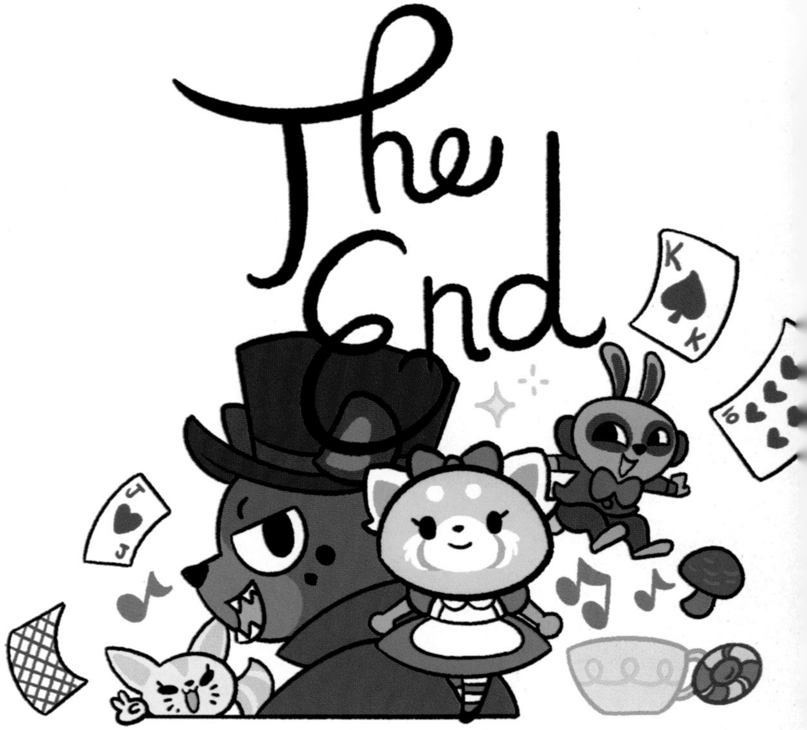
The End

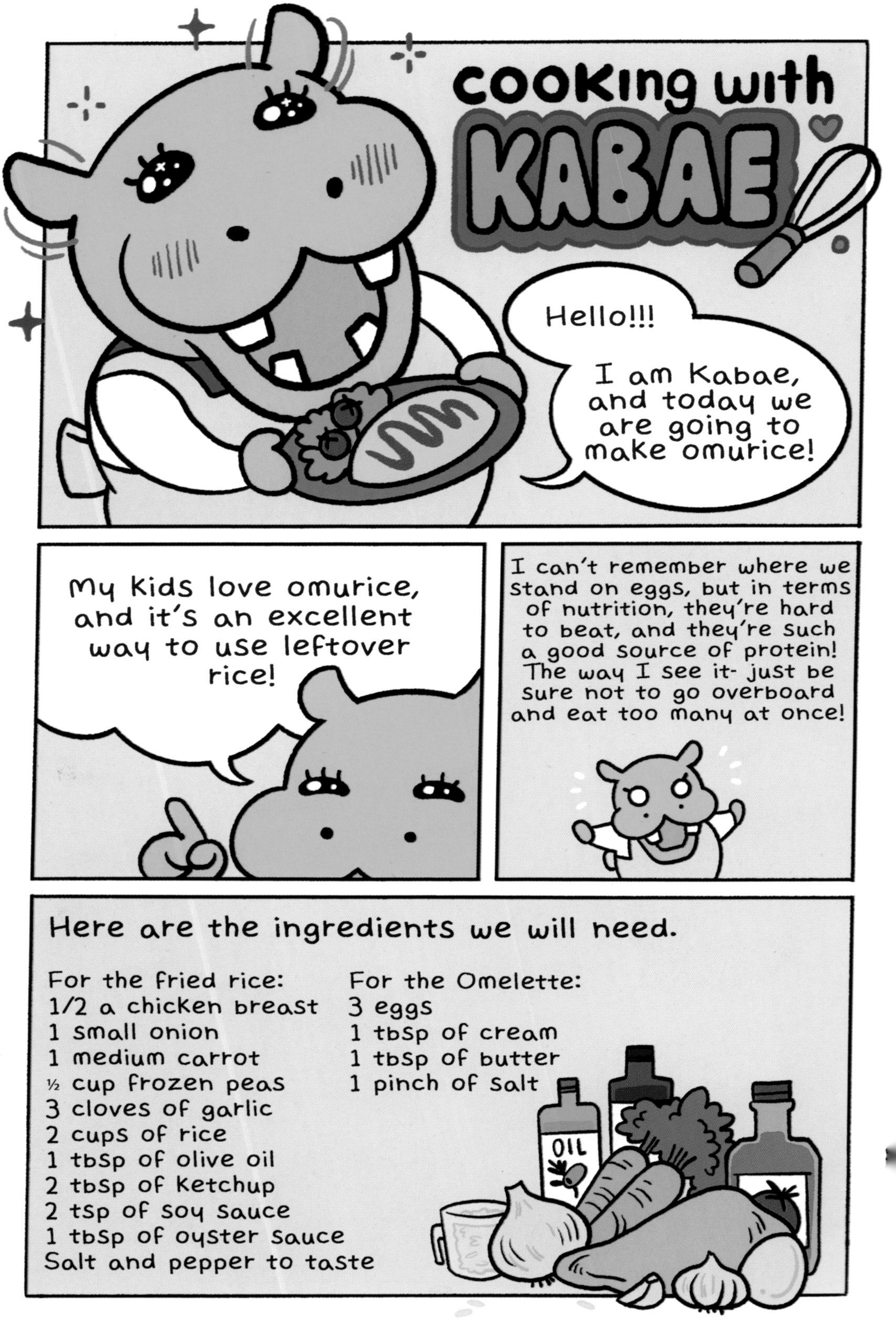

COOKING WITH
KABAE
Hello!!!
I am Kabae, and today we are going to make omurice!
My kids love omurice, and it's an excellent way to use leftover rice!
I can't remember where we stand on eggs, but in terms of nutrition, they're hard to beat, and they're such a good source of protein! The way I see it- just be sure not to go overboard and eat too many at once!
Here are the ingredients we will need.
For the fried rice:
1/2 a chicken breast
1 small onion
1 medium carrot
½ cup frozen peas
3 cloves of garlic
2 cups of rice
1 tbsp of olive oil
2 tbsp of ketchup
2 tsp of soy sauce
1 tbsp of oyster sauce
Salt and pepper to taste
For the Omelette:
3 eggs
1 tbsp of cream
1 tbsp of butter
1 pinch of salt
OIL

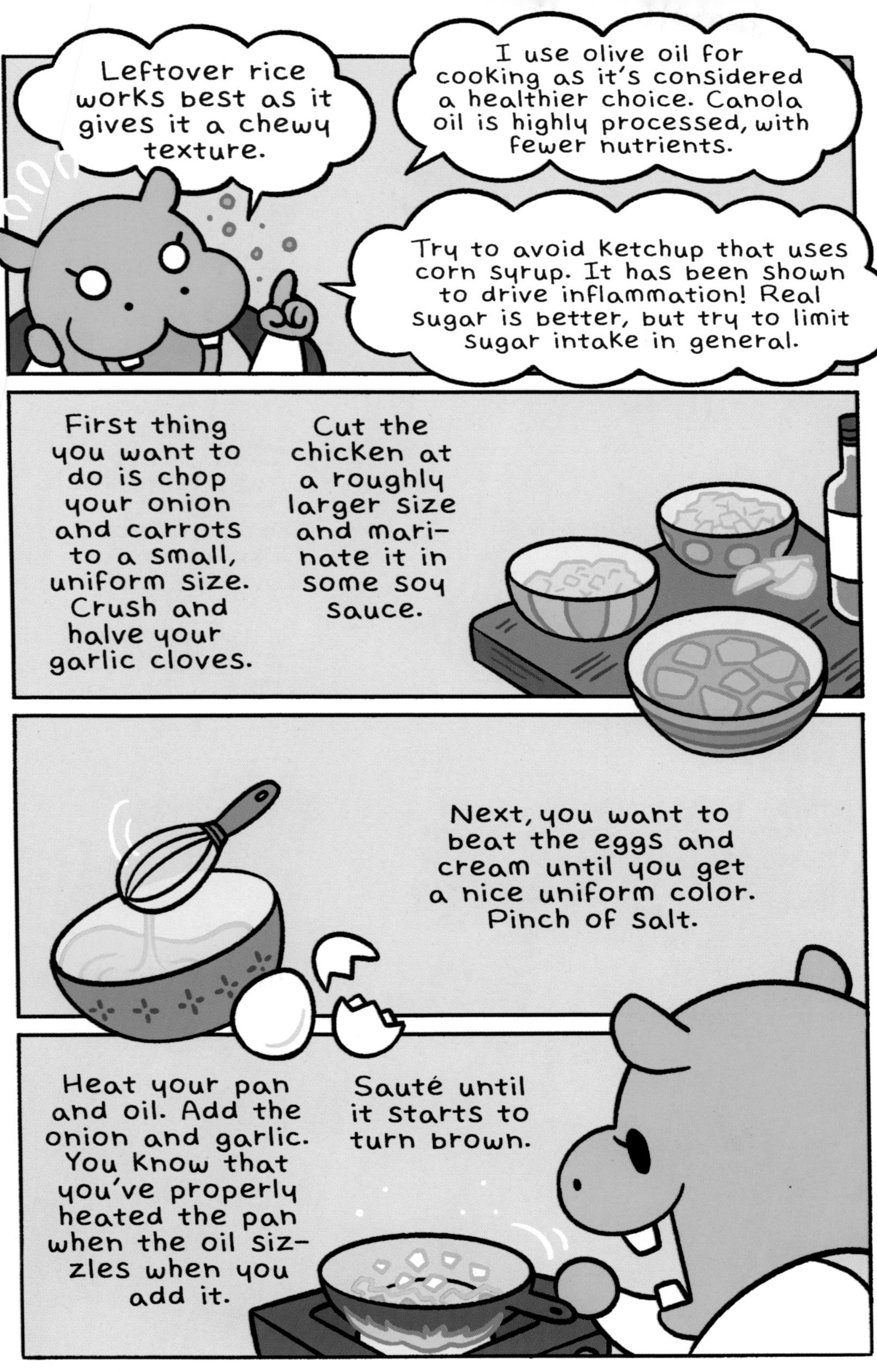

Leftover rice works best as it gives it a chewy texture.
I use olive oil for cooking as it's considered a healthier choice. Canola oil is highly processed, with fewer nutrients.
Try to avoid ketchup that uses corn syrup. It has been shown to drive inflammation! Real sugar is better, but try to limit sugar intake in general.
First thing you want to do is chop your onion and carrots to a small, uniform size. Crush and halve your garlic cloves.
Cut the chicken at a roughly larger size and marinate it in some soy sauce.
Next, you want to beat the eggs and cream until you get a nice uniform color. Pinch of salt.
Heat your pan and oil. Add the onion and garlic. You know that you've properly heated the pan when the oil sizzles when you add it.
Sauté until it starts to turn brown.

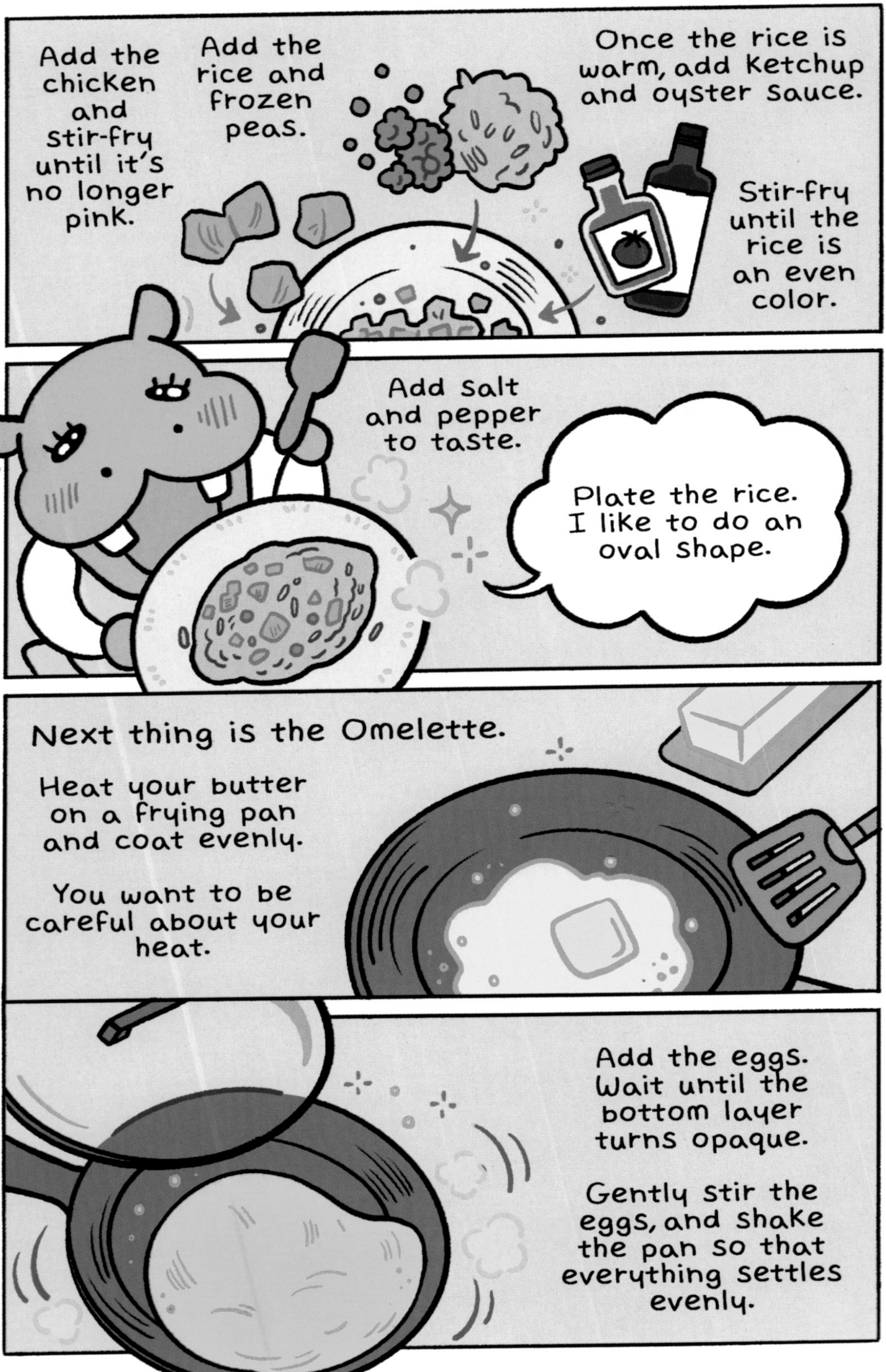
Add the chicken and stir-fry until it's no longer pink.
Add the rice and frozen peas.
Once the rice is warm, add ketchup and oyster sauce.
Stir-fry until the rice is an even color.
Add salt and pepper to taste.
Plate the rice. I like to do an oval shape.
Next thing is the Omelette.
Heat your butter on a frying pan and coat evenly.
You want to be careful about your heat.
Add the eggs. Wait until the bottom layer turns opaque.
Gently stir the eggs, and shake the pan so that everything settles evenly.

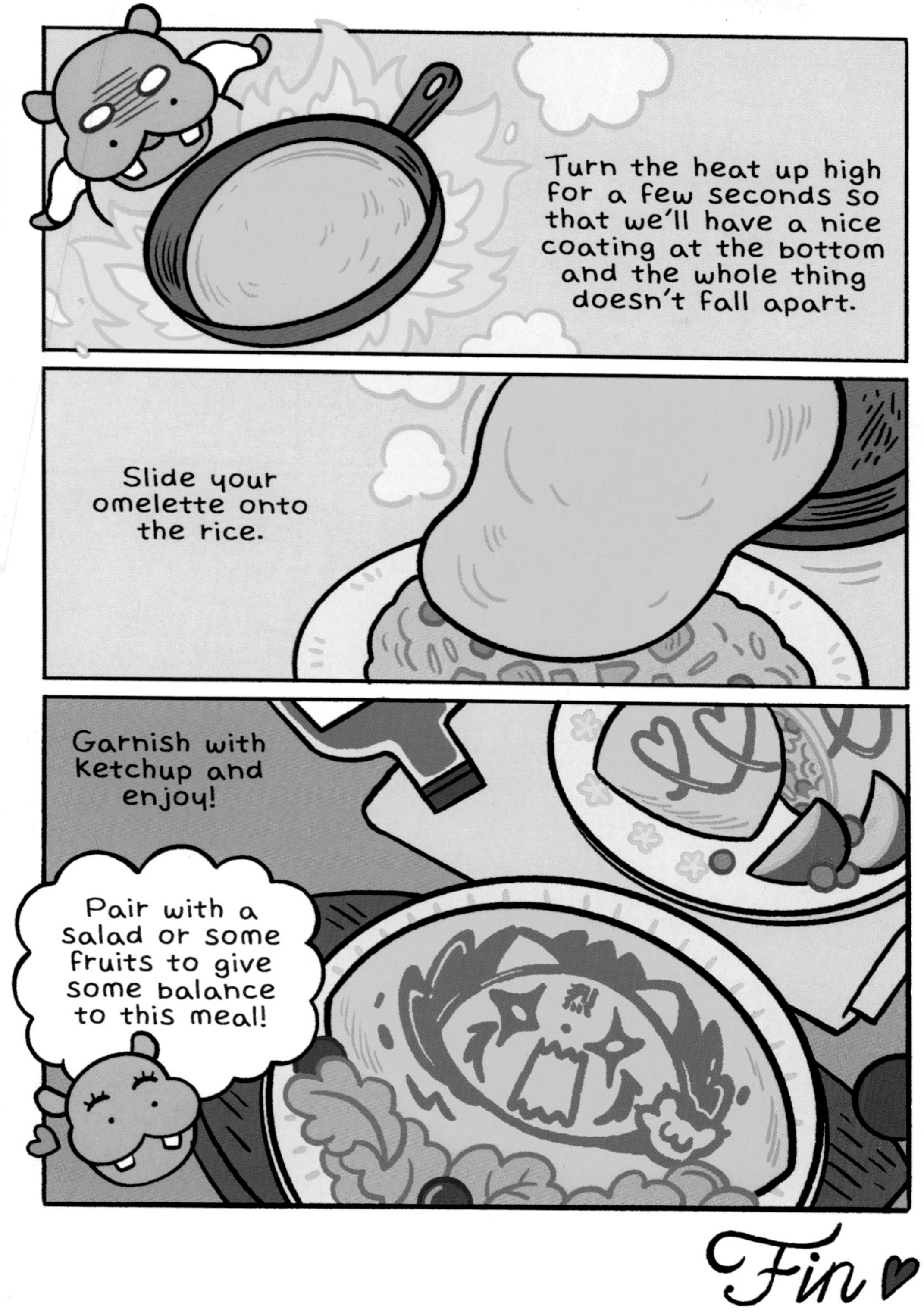
Turn the heat up high for a few seconds so that we'll have a nice coating at the bottom and the whole thing doesn't fall apart.
Slide your omelette onto the rice.
Garnish with ketchup and enjoy!
Pair with a salad or some fruits to give some balance to this meal!

Fin ♥

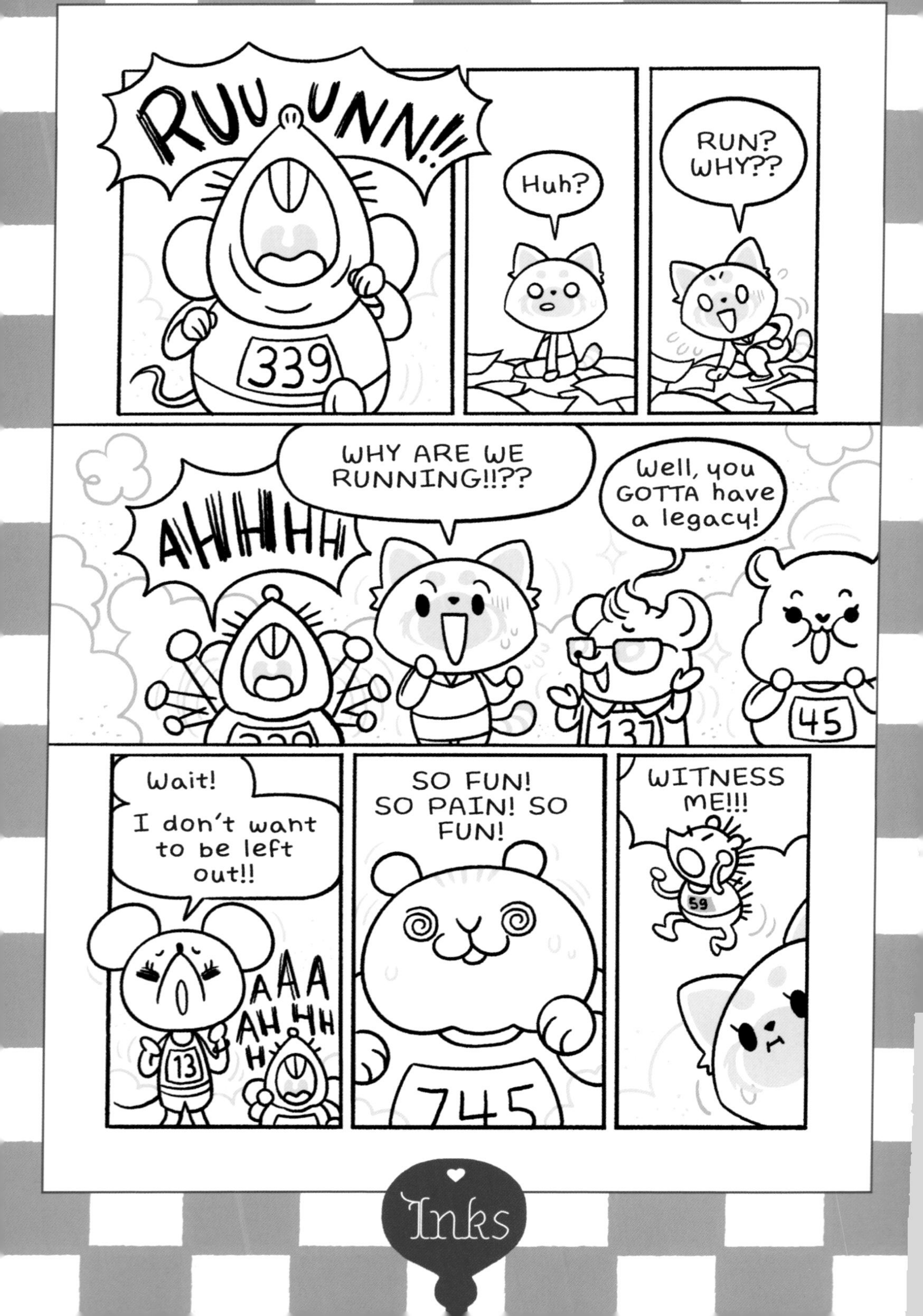
RUU UNN!!
Huh?
RUN? WHY??
AHHHHH
WHY ARE WE RUNNING!!??
Well, you GOTTA have a legacy!
Wait!
I don't want to be left out!!
AAAAHHHH
SO FUN! SO PAIN! SO FUN!
WITNESS ME!!!

Inks

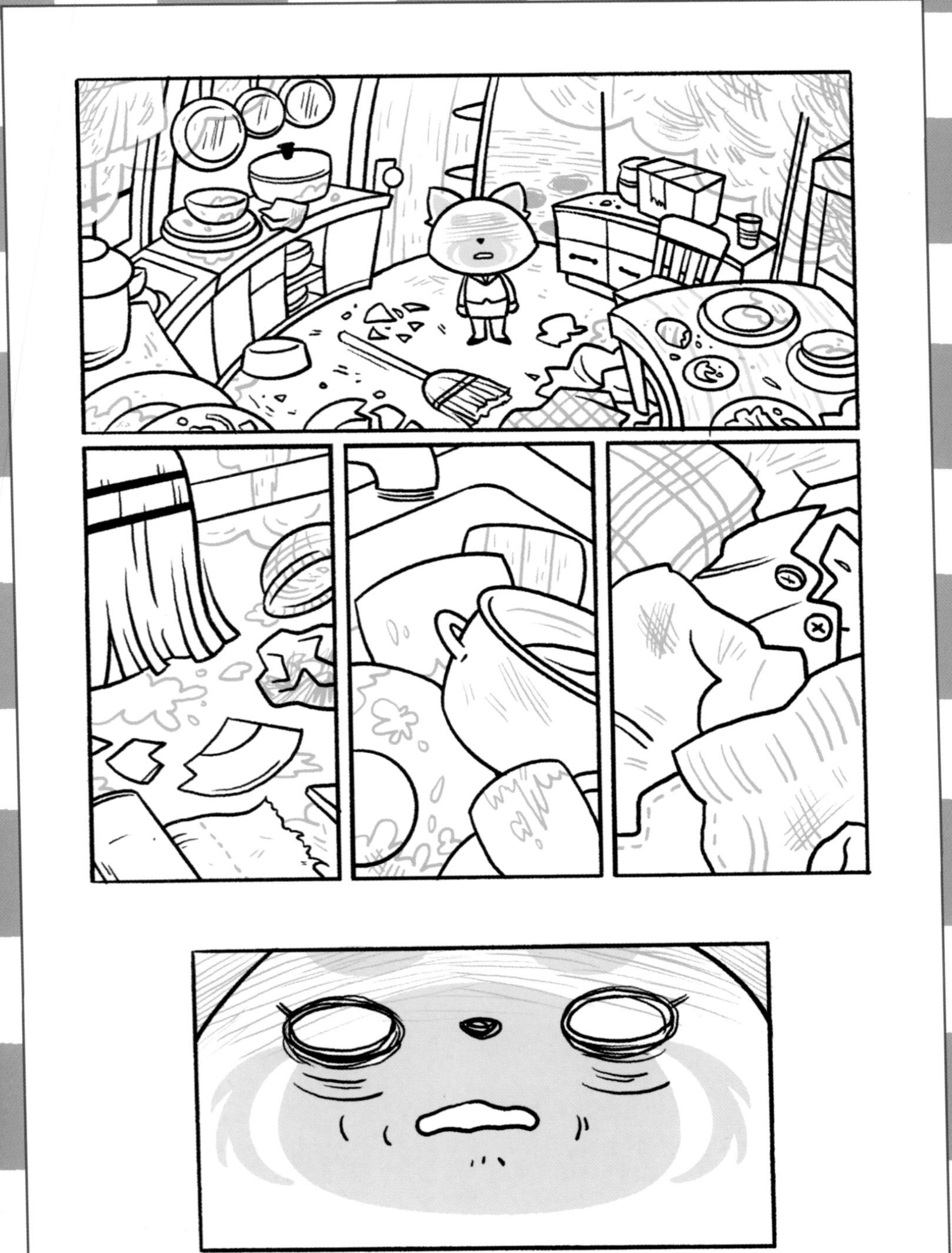

Inks

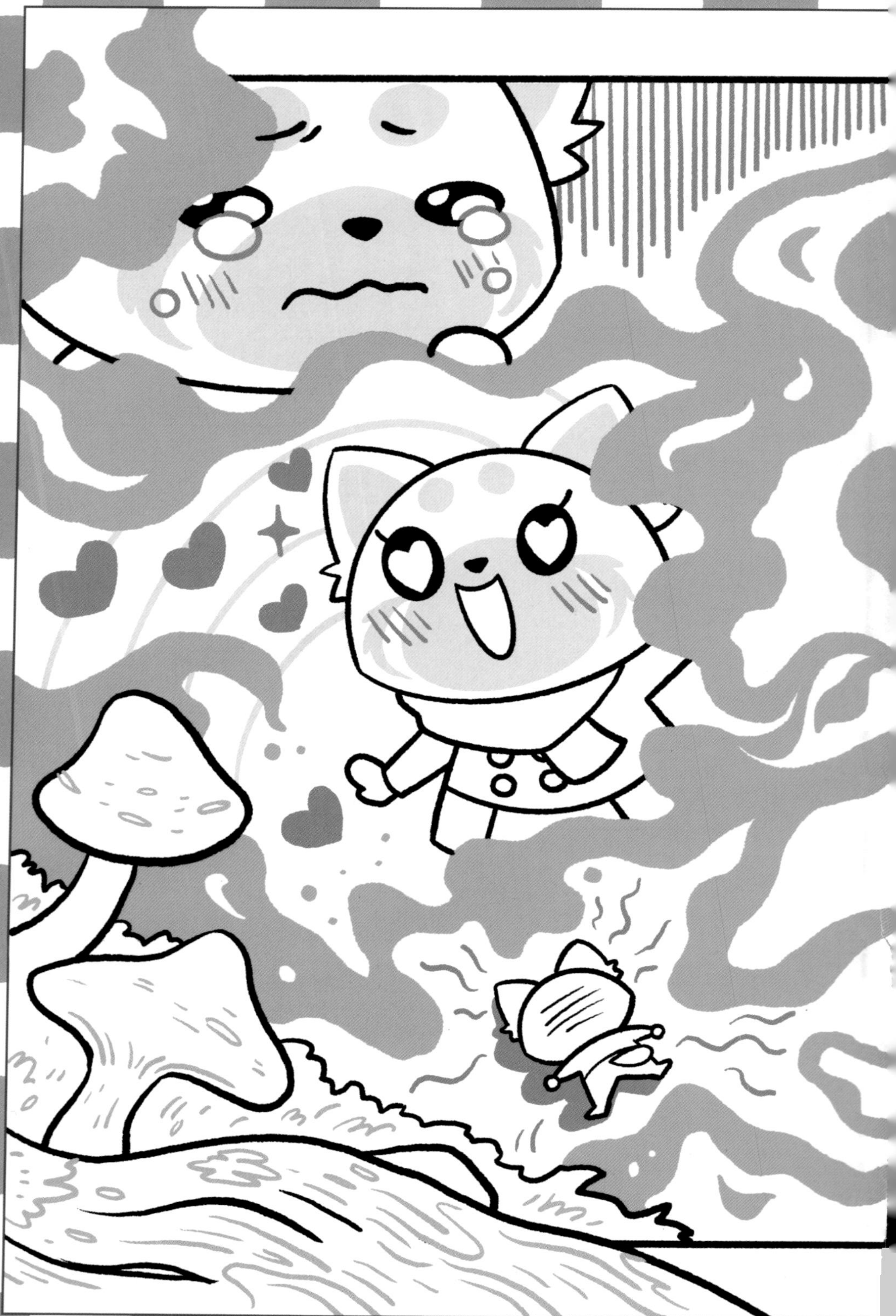

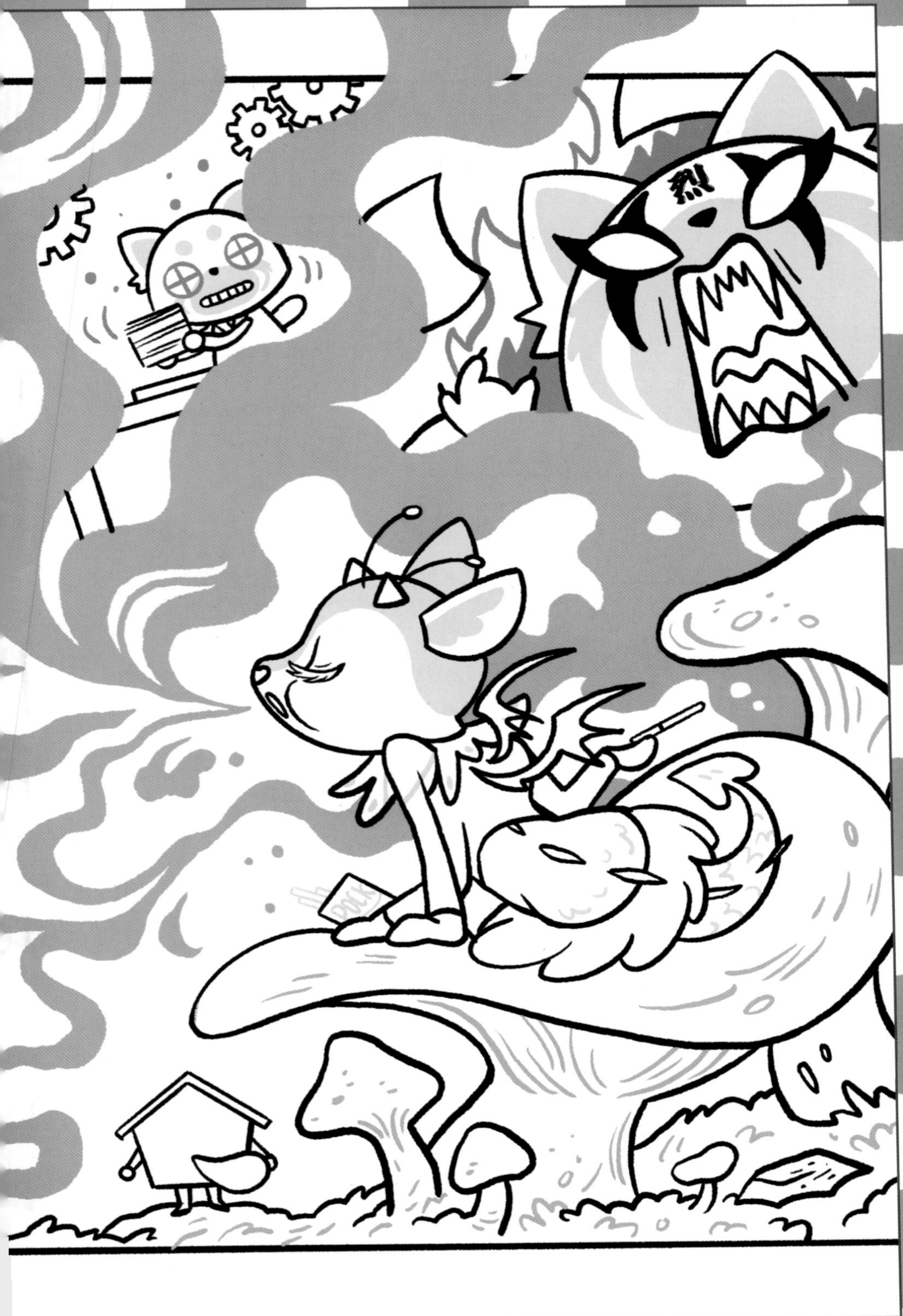

烈

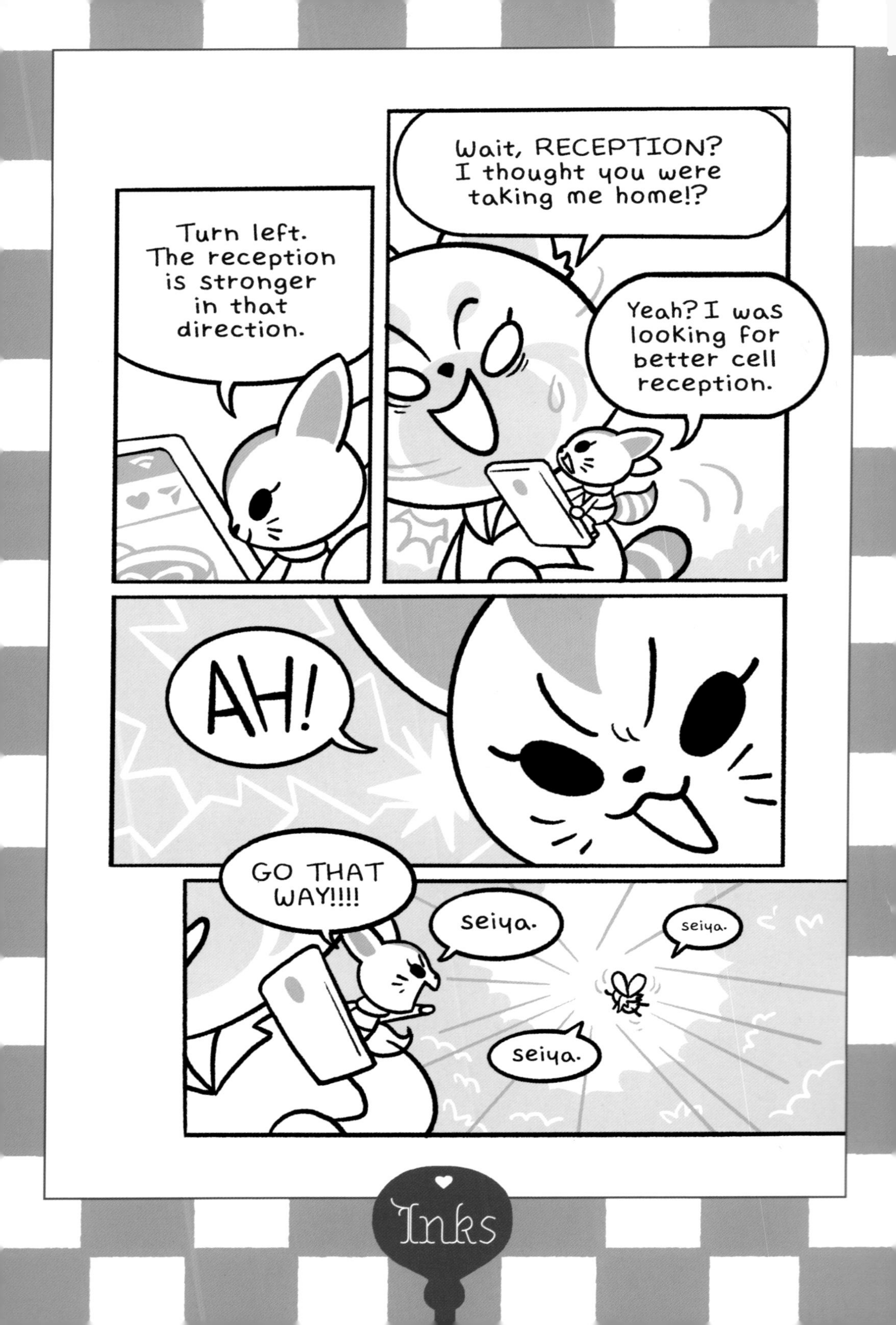
Turn left. The reception is stronger in that direction.
Wait, RECEPTION? I thought you were taking me home!?
Yeah? I was looking for better cell reception.
AH!
GO THAT WAY!!!!
seiya.
seiya.
seiya.

Inks

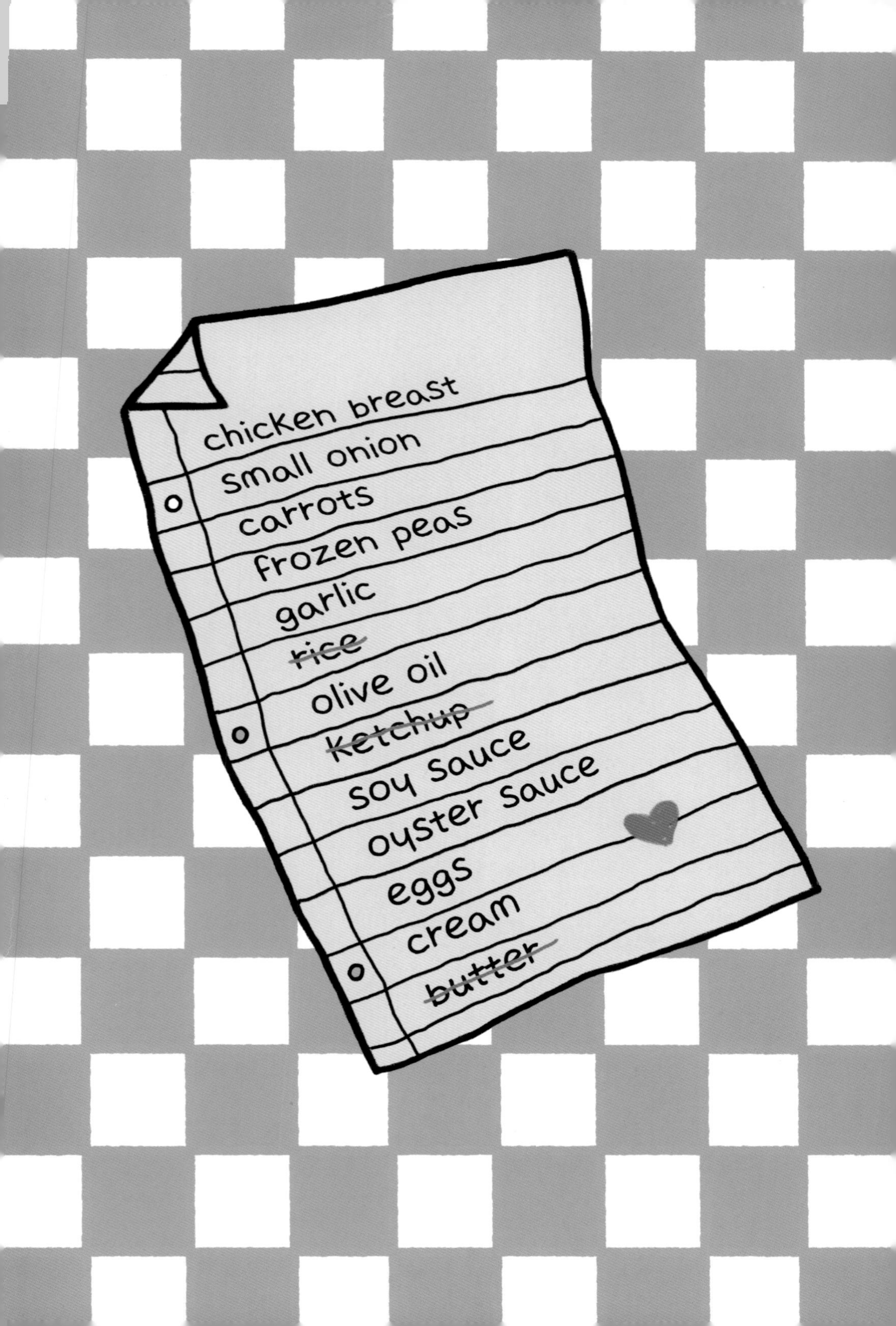
chicken breast
small onion
carrots
frozen peas
garlic
rice
olive oil
ketchup
soy sauce
oyster sauce
eggs
cream
butter

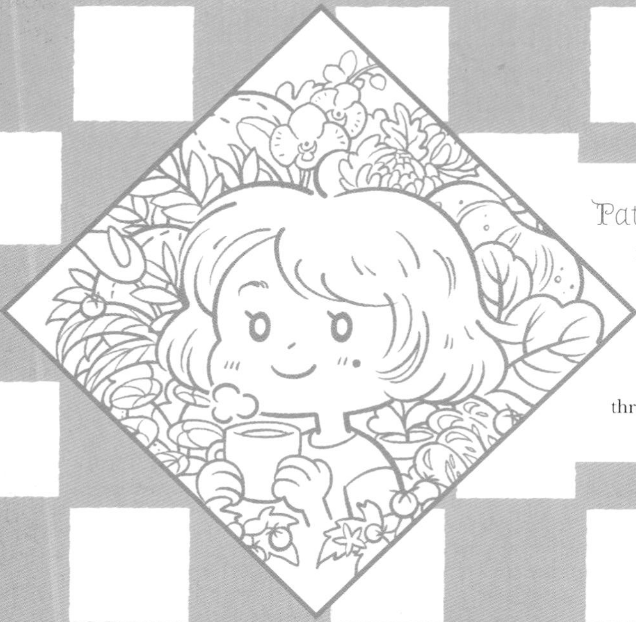

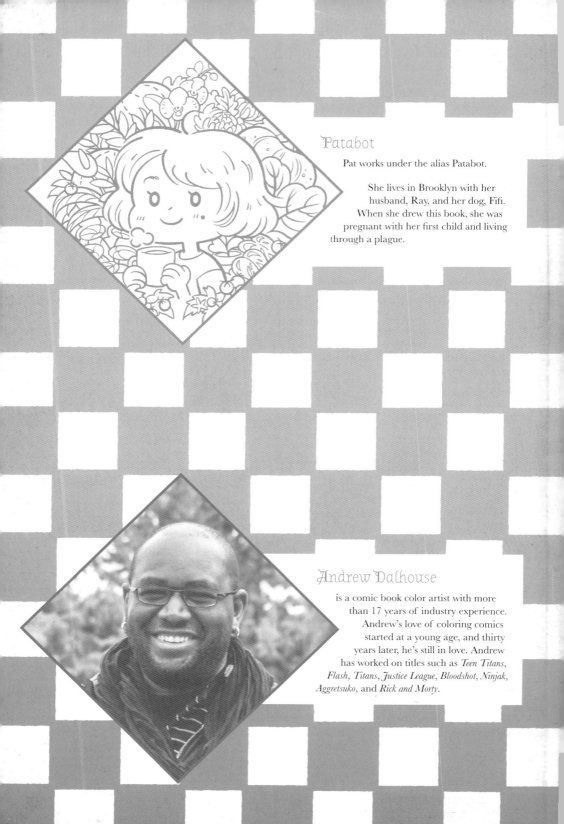

Patabot

Pat works under the alias Patabot.

She lives in Brooklyn with her husband, Ray, and her dog, Fifi. When she drew this book, she was pregnant with her first child and living through a plague.

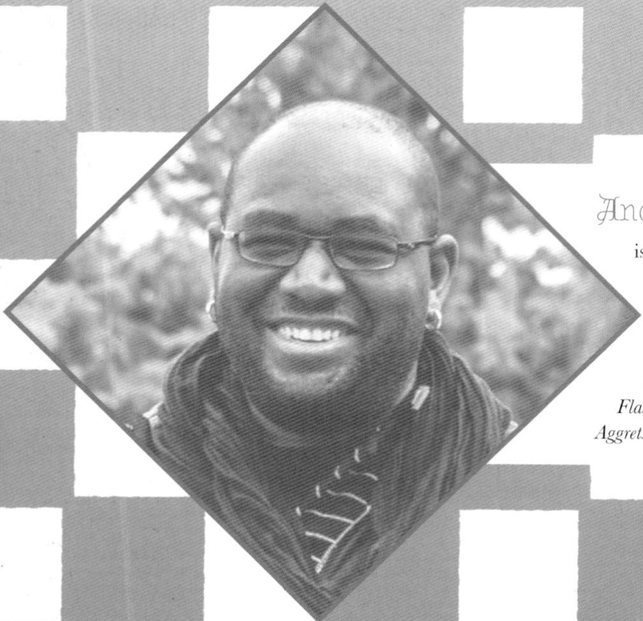

Andrew Dalhouse

is a comic book color artist with more than 17 years of industry experience. Andrew's love of coloring comics started at a young age, and thirty years later, he's still in love. Andrew has worked on titles such as *Teen Titans*, *Flash*, *Titans*, *Justice League*, *Bloodshot*, *Ninjak*, *Aggretsuko*, and *Rick and Morty*.

Join Aggretsuko

as she navigates the chaos of her life and work, with only her heavy metal karaoke rage to help her through!

Aggretsuko
WORK / RAGE BALANCE

Aggretsuko
Little Rei of Sunshine

Aggretsuko
meet her friends

ONI PRESS

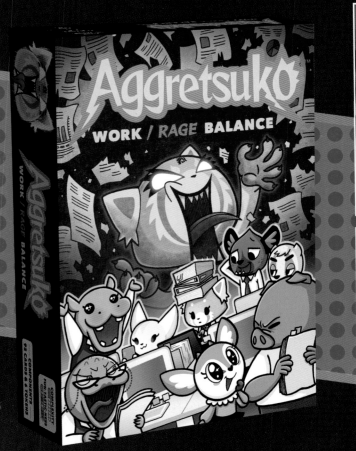

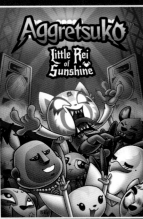

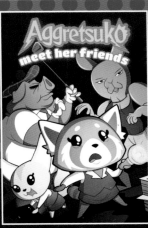

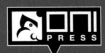

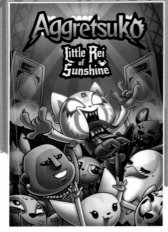

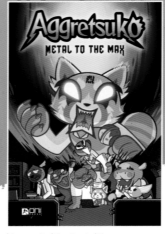

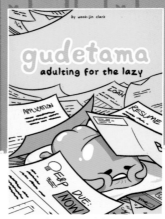

Aggretsuko
Little Rei of Sunshine

Aggretsuko
METAL TO THE MAX

by wook-jin clark
gudetama
adulting for the lazy
LOAN
APPLICATION
RESUME
DUE:
NOW

Aggretsuko: Little Rei of Sunshine

By Brenda Hickey

Retsuko and friends have to fight for their right to party in a METAL vs. METAL vocal battle that pits Retsuko against a shadowy enemy.

Aggretsuko: Metal to the Max

By Daniel Barnes, D.J. Kirkland, Jarrett Williams, and Brenda Hickey

Retsuko, the highly-relatable red panda and star of Netflix's *Aggretsuko*, stars in three all-new comic tales of office madness!

Gudetama: Adulting for The Lazy

By Wook-Jin Clark

Get over your fear of responsibility with Gudetama, the laziest of eggs.

Read more from Oni Press!

THE BLACK·MAGE
DANIEL BARNES • D.J. KIRKLAND

"Mooncakes is spellbinding!"
Mooncakes
Wendy Xu
Suzanne Walker

Dream Daddy
a Dad Dating Comic Book

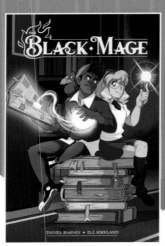

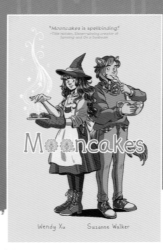

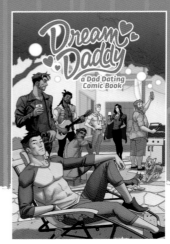

Black Mage

By Daniel Barnes and D.J. Kirkland

When a historically white wizarding school opens its doors to its first-ever black student, everyone believes that the wizarding community is finally taking its first crucial steps toward inclusivity. Or is it?

Mooncakes

By Suzanne Walker and Wendy Xu

A story of love and demons, family and witchcraft.

Dream Daddy: A Dad Dating Comic Book

By Various

Oni Press presents Dream Daddy, a comics series based on the acclaimed Game Grumps visual novel video game!

For more information on these and other fine Oni Press comic books and graphic novels, visit www.onipress.com.